THE *Hellhound's* UnCHRISTMAS MIRACLE

THE *Hellhound's* UnCHRISTMAS MIRACLE

MARIE CARDNO
WRITING AS
ZOE CHANT

I

FLEANCE

C hildren were crying, and it was all Fleance's fault.

Fleance's pack alpha, Caine Guinness, rubbed his jaw. Caine's eyes were shadowed with exhaustion, and bright with the hint of his inner hellhound's careful gaze. "Tell me again what happened."

What happened is that "careful" isn't a word you could ever use to describe my hellhound. Fleance gritted his teeth and sat back. He was in the small staff room at the Puppy Express, a tourist retreat where he and the rest of the pack worked part-time to get them out of Caine and his mate Meaghan's hair. Meaghan was expecting twins and had made it extremely clear that her pack's instincts to wait on her hand and foot were *not* the way to make her happy.

Caine being called in to deal with Fleance's hellhound like a parent being called to the principal's office? Not part of the plan.

Now, more than ever, Fleance felt like a poor imitation of the alpha who had saved his life. With his powerful frame, dark red hair, and piercing blue eyes, Caine drew attention wherever he went. Fleance's hair was a lighter red, his eyes a paler gray-blue, and even though Caine had been turned into a hellhound years after Fleance, he'd managed to do the one thing Fleance had always thought was impossible: break free of the alpha who turned him. A year and a half ago, Caine had wrestled control of the pack away from Angus Parker and broken the chains around Fleance and the other two members of the pack. And now...

The sound of the panic he'd caused outside would have been inaudible to a human, but it grated against Fleance's enhanced shifter hearing. And his conscience.

Why are you angry? his hellhound asked from inside his head, smoke dripping from its words as it watched him suspiciously. *We won!*

You call that 'winning'? Kids crying because you swamped them with your fear magic?

Yes! They will not hurt anyone again!

Fleance's jaw went tight. He pushed his hellhound's thoughts away and repeated what he'd already told Caine when he arrived. "One of the kids yanked on a dog's tail."

"That's all?"

"That's all it took. My hellhound wanted to hunt it down. It—" Fleance frowned, trying to trace the logic under his hellhound's rage.

The Puppy Express was one of the main tourist attractions in Pine Valley, the small mountain town where Fleance's pack lived. The Express maintained a web of sled dog trails that wound through the forest at the edge of town and hired out teams of dogs to do what they loved best: run. There were jingle-bell-bedecked sleighs in winter, and Fleance and the other hellhounds had spent the slushy shoulder season repainting the summer sleds.

It was a sanctuary. The Express, Pine Valley, every goddamned pine needle and puddle of snowmelt in the place. Fleance didn't like to think about his life before Pine Valley, but what he'd found here was nothing short of a miracle. Friends. Colleagues. A life he could be proud of.

Or so he'd thought. Dread clawed at his throat, following the lines of the thin scars he'd never be free of. He should have known it was too good to be true. Too good for *him*. His hellhound had spent the first years of its existence acting as an enforcer for the evil alpha who had turned him, and now whenever it sensed someone stepping out of line, it attacked. What sort of a monster turned on little kids for playing up?

"This isn't the first time you've had this problem with your hellhound, but I thought you had it under control." Caine rubbed his jaw, his fingers scraping on the stubble, and guilt shot through Fleance's gut.

He schooled his face and his heart before anything could show. He was already causing his alpha enough problems; he didn't want Caine to pick up on the true depth of his feelings via his pack-sense. The man had better things to do than deal with his problems.

"Rhys and I have been working on it," he said. Rhys was another member of the pack. Where Fleance saw his hellhound as a curse, Rhys saw it as a puzzle—one he could break. "I haven't had any outbursts for weeks and I—I thought I'd be safe working the till. I wouldn't go out on the trails, there's too much potential for things to go wrong, but I thought inside would be… safe."

"And how'd that work out?" Caine muttered. He raised a hand and grimaced apologetically as Fleance started to answer. "That was a rhetorical question, Flea."

Fleance shrugged away a momentary unease at the nickname. "My hellhound says it wants to stop people being hurt." The words came out as an embarrassed half-growl. "But ever since Christmas it sees threats everywhere."

"…Yes." Caine gave him a searching look, which Flea accepted warily. He wasn't sure how much Caine could feel of his thoughts, but he trusted he'd never pick into his brain for them.

Not like his first alpha.

Fleance shivered, and tried to pass it off as another shrug. When Caine still didn't say anything, more words forced themselves past Fleance's lips. "Something doesn't make sense."

He didn't have Rhys's talent for figuring things out, but something about this latest horror wasn't right. His hellhound snarled softly, and he hushed it. *Caine is our alpha. A good alpha. We can trust him.* He went on, piecing his thoughts together word by word: "Rhys's theory is that my hellhound wants to protect people. Last Christmas, it went crazy when that couple went off-trail in the snow, because they were putting themselves in danger. But a kid pulling a dog's tail? What's the worst that can happen, that scaring the hell out of some poor five-year-old is the better option? It doesn't feel like I'm protecting anyone."

"No." Caine's voice was calm, but his eyes were watching Fleance too carefully for him to be entirely at ease. "It sounds more like it's punishing them."

Yes! Make them pay! Make it RIGHT!

Fleance flinched. Caine's eyes widened and he leaned back, hands raised. "Easy."

Anger flared inside Fleance. *His* anger, not his hellhound's. *Why are you wasting time talking? Why not fix this yourself?* Fleance swallowed hard over the bile that rose in his throat. Caine wasn't that sort of alpha. Fleance didn't *want* him to be that sort of alpha. He'd spent too long under the boot of a man who used his alpha powers to cage and control him. But now, with this…

He clenched his fists on the torn fabric on the chair's arms, then released them slowly.

"You were in Parker's pack the longest out of the three of you, weren't you?"

Fleance's eye twitched. Had Caine read his mind?

No, he told himself. He'd just cut straight to the point, like usual.

He dropped his head. "I was the first one he turned. His *test subject*, Rhys calls me." Fleance resisted the urge to touch the bite scars on his neck. Across from him, Caine's knuckles went white as he gripped his upper thigh, where his own turning scar was. "You think he got something wrong when he turned me." His voice was flat. "My hellhound's broken. That's why it's so violent now that I'm not under Parker's control."

Caine made a face. "I don't think that. And I've known Angus Parker since I was at college, remember. Given the way he treated the three of you when you were his pack, I doubt he'd consider violence to be something *wrong* with you."

"Is that meant to make me feel better?"

"Yes and no?" Caine's lips curved in a wry half-smile. "Yes, reassuring, because whatever you've been telling yourself, you're not a monster.

I spent long enough thinking I was one, so I should know. And no, not reassuring, because like I said. I know Parker. Not as well as I'd thought, but from what Rhys and Manu have told me..." He sat back and rubbed his face. "This is my fault."

"What?" Fleance was still managing his reaction to the news Caine had been talking to Rhys and Manu. All those years with Parker had trained him to keep his problems secret. His surprise that Caine thought this was *his* fault slipped onto his face.

"I'm your alpha, aren't I? I'm meant to take responsibility for all of you."

Strange way of saying 'control', Fleance thought before he could stop himself, as Caine kept talking.

"I should have seen you weren't coping. I should have done something to help. I've been so distracted with Meaghan's pregnancy. We knew it would change things, the Heartwells warned us about that, but now..."

A shiver rippled across Fleance's pack-sense. He leaned forward, trying to trace the source of the disturbance, and gasped.

Fleance had always been keenly aware of his pack. When it was just Parker, there had been no escaping it: his alpha had been like a black hole, dragging at his attention and ready to lash out if he felt he wasn't being shown due respect. When Parker had added Rhys and Manu to the pack, the black hole had been joined by two other circling stars—caught in its orbit, always at risk of being eaten alive.

Two Christmases ago, Caine had defeated Parker in combat. Suddenly, the black hole had vanished. Now, when Fleance closed his eyes and looked inside himself, past his hellhound's smoke-filled den, he saw a constellation of lights whirling through a black night sky. Still caught in orbit, but no longer crushed into place by a cruel alpha's control.

That was what made Pine Valley so precious to Fleance, and Christmas even more so. It felt like a charmed place and time. The longer he spent there the more true that seemed, as he learned about the other miracles the town had experienced each Christmas season. The Christmas before he'd moved to Pine Valley, one of the local dragon clan had found his mate, breaking a curse that would have forced him to lose either his dragon or his human side forever. Then, Caine had met his mate, and broken Parker's control over his pack. And again, last Christmas, another piece of magic. Two more hearts made whole.

In Pine Valley, Fleance felt safe for the first time since he was a teenager. He didn't need to keep one eye on his pack-sense at all times, and this must have been why he never noticed the newest changes to his psychic night sky.

Two new points of light, barely pinpricks against the darkness, whirled near the central star, around the shining moon that represented Caine's mate. Fleance blinked—and there was another rippling shiver, and they were gone.

Two almost-there new pack members. *Twins.*

Fleance's eyes flew open and he met Caine's tired gaze. "They're hellhounds? Without being bitten?"

"Seems that way." Caine became agitated. "And Abigail's been telling Meaghan about things that changed for her after she had Ruby, and there's going to be two of them, and... It's going to be a lot." His eyes went glassy. "A *lot.*"

And he doesn't need an uncontrolled, violent, broken hellhound to deal with on top of all that. Fleance gritted his jaw. "This isn't your fault," he told his alpha. "It's—I can handle it. I *will* handle it. And if worse comes to worst—"

He reached towards the central star in the constellation that represented his pack. Almost invisible against the darkness were the threads of power that linked him to his alpha. They were only threads, not the coiling, choking chains Parker had used to control his lackeys. But they were there. "You can make me stop."

"It won't come to that," Caine replied.

"You don't know that."

Caine levelled his gaze at him. His hellhound's fire moved behind his eyes, assessing. *Thinking.* Fleance forced himself not to show his discomfort.

Then Caine sighed, ran his fingers through his dark-red locks, and stood up. "Sounds like they're finished out there," he said. "Bob's taken the tourists off into the trails, and Rhys and Manu ran at the first sign of trouble like the sensible bastards they are. No one left to cause you any trouble."

Fleance didn't mention that the reason the other hellhounds had vanished like smoke was that they were afraid they'd catch his hellhound's rage. It was contagious; he might not be an alpha, but something in his hellhound's hunting instinct lit a similar instinct in the others.

Thank God for Caine, he thought, standing up. He would hide himself away in a cabin if he needed to. Pine Valley had plenty of hunting lodges, farther out in the mountains where you'd have to run for days to meet another soul. But having Caine's alpha authority as a backup if everything else went wrong...

He'd never thought he'd come to consider his chains with relief. But he'd never thought he'd be free of Parker, either.

"Let's get a move on. I'm driving Meaghan down to town for her ob-gyn appointment this afternoon." Caine paused at the door. *Hmm.*

The voice in his head was Caine's, but the rumble underlaying it was all hellhound. Fleance bowed his head. Caine was his alpha, and he was a good one, but Fleance knew from bitter experience how these things worked. If his alpha said jump, you didn't wait to hear how high. If your alpha said *hmm*, you kept your mouth shut until he finished thinking.

Caine stared at him coolly over his shoulder. "Before we go… one more thing."

He walked over to the safe that held the Puppy Express's cash earnings for the week and pushed his hand through the door of it. The metal shimmered around his wrist as he used his hellhound powers to make it as insubstantial as mist.

When he withdrew his hand, he was holding a stack of bills. Fleance watched as he casually pocketed them.

"What are you—" He broke off as his hellhound reared up inside him, all fire and rage. Smoke curled at the edges of his vision. If he looked in a mirror, he knew his eyes would have transformed from their usual mild gray-blue into pits of spitting hellfire.

His hellhound held back—barely. Caine was his alpha. Fleance couldn't even conceive of his hellhound attacking his alpha. But…

His hellhound snarled, a low, fierce rumble that made Fleance's vision blur.

Fleance sat down again and dug his fingers into the arms of the chair. Worn vinyl cracked beneath his fingertips. No, not fingertips. *Claws.*

"Boss," he forced out. Caine shot him a smile that said *we're-all-friends-here* and patted his pocket.

"Let's head out," he said, his voice casual. "I'll escort you back to the house, and let the others know they're on the hook for your shifts until we've figured this out."

"But you're—" Fleance broke off as his throat went dry.

Caine was leaving with the cash in his jacket pocket. And even though Fleance knew this was some sort of trick, a *test*, and because he knew it his hellhound should too, the beast inside him was howling with rage.

Its voice thundered in his skull. *No!* it howled. *Not this time! We won't let him get away with it!*

Fleance leaped up, unable to stop himself. His hellhound was tearing his way out of him, forcing a shift that would—

"All right, that's enough."

Caine's alpha authority wound like chains around Fleance's limbs. His hellhound stopped. Its rage was still there, but contained within the power of his alpha's command. Fleance's chest heaved as he gasped in air. He dropped back into his seat like a puppet whose strings had been cut.

"That proves one thing," Caine said, grinning. Fleance stared at him. Had he gone mad? "Don't worry, Flea. I might not like to use them, but if my alpha powers mean I can stop you from—"

Not this time! Fleance's hellhound roared. *Make him—stop him—our alpha should not—*

The rest of its words were lost in a storm of brimstone-laden fire. Fleance's spine cracked and he fell forward as his shift took hold. Muscles burning, he tried desperately to catch hold of his hellhound, but the creature of smoke and flame evaded his grasp. He transformed in a blaze of fear and rage.

Fear poured from him. It sent tendrils out to choke the breath of anyone it could find, to drive sharp fingertips into spines and the backs of necks, to make shadows dance at the edges of vision, to make every breath seem shallower than the last. Once it found its prey it would stick to them like a tick, scaring them into running. The hunt would begin.

It found Caine.

Transformed, Fleance's hellhound filled the small staff room. He loomed over his still-human alpha, panting out smoke. The urge to hunt flooded through Fleance's veins: his hellhound's primary instinct, primal and unstoppable.

Villain—monster—stop him—protect—

His hellhound's voice howled through Fleance's head, screaming words that were disconnected but pulled together by its bonfire rage.

Stop this! he commanded. His words disappeared like tissue paper held to a flame.

His hellhound prowled forward, placing its massive paws carefully, heavily. The floor hissed, smoke rising from under his claws.

Don't do this, Fleance. Caine was still in his human form, but his voice packed a punch like a freight train. Surely his hellhound couldn't ignore it.

His hellhound took another step forward.

Awareness crackled at the edge of Fleance's mind: the rest of the pack. Manu and Rhys, the two younger hellhounds, were back at the Guinnesses' lodge. Fleance's urge to hunt singed the edges of their minds, a match flame to kindling. The huskies left in the kennels started to howl, and the ones Bob had taken out with the kids stopped in their tracks, shivering with anticipation.

Caine didn't back away. Fleance felt his hellhound's frustration: it wanted to hunt, to *chase*. It couldn't chase someone who wouldn't run.

He's our alpha! Fleance yelled inside his head. *Stop this!*

Closer—harder to find, her human mind not burning like the hellhounds' did but shining like the moon, with two precious lights in close orbit around it—his alpha's mate. Meaghan. Caine swore under his breath.

They're too small to hunt, Fleance's hellhound snarled. *Too small to protect themselves. If the alpha won't, the pack must—MAKE HIM STOP! WE WON'T LET IT HAPPEN AGAIN!*

Caine shot Fleance a look that came close to dangerous, took the cash out of his pocket and tossed it back at the safe. Without his hellhound magic, it bounced off the door and fell to the floor. He swore—out loud this time—and ducked to pick it up.

Fleance relaxed as his alpha pushed the stolen bills back into the safe. *There,* he told his hellhound. *Happy now?*

Acceptable. Goosebumps prickled on the back of Fleance's neck. His hellhound sank back on its haunches, out of its threatening stance. *If he doesn't do it again.*

"This is not good," Caine remarked. He didn't sound upset. More... resigned. He rubbed his forehead, exhaustion pulling at the corners of his mouth. "If I could control you, that would be one thing, but... It's been getting worse since Christmas, you said? And Meaghan's due at the end of the month. We'll have to—damn." His voice lowered. "I wish this shit came with a manual."

Fleance shifted back. He managed to pull his clothes back with him, but they were torn and ragged.

"No," he said, panting. "This is what I needed. I know what's wrong with my hellhound now."

Caine shot him a sharp look and Fleance swallowed.

"It's Parker," he said.

It all made sense now. His hellhound wasn't attacking 'criminals' for no reason—it was still reacting against everything that had happened under its previous alpha. All those years of being forced to hurt people for his alpha's profit had broken something inside him.

Caine fixed him with a serious look. "Parker's gone. I cut him loose. He's not here and he's not a part of this pack. No one here is in any danger from him."

Not true! Not true! His hellhound wasn't growling now. It was whimpering. Desperate.

Fleance was used to keeping his thoughts off his face. He didn't let Caine see anything of the dread that pooled in his veins.

Parker might be gone, but the danger wasn't. No wonder his hellhound was so frantic.

Sure, Caine had cut Angus Parker off. The former alpha was no longer a part of the Guinness pack. But he hadn't *stopped* him. Fleance felt sick. Caine had taken over the pack and banished Parker from ever returning to Pine Valley, but that didn't prevent him from doing to other people what he'd done to Fleance and the others.

No wonder his hellhound was going mad. Ever since he'd been turned, Fleance had hated being under his uncle's control. And now that he was free, he'd done nothing to save other people from the same fate. Meaghan announcing her pregnancy must have been the straw that broke the camel's back. Even if the chances of Parker returning to Pine Valley and fighting Caine for leadership of the pack were close to nil, the risk was too high.

Besides, Fleance knew Parker. Banishment wouldn't keep him away forever. He'd find a way to come back, and he'd make it hurt. Fleance knew that better than anyone, because Parker was more than just Fleance's former alpha. He was his uncle. Pack was different to family... but not completely. Not enough that Fleance could trust that he wasn't the weak link in the Guinnesses' pack.

And until he knew there was no chance that Parker would come back and take advantage of that connection, Fleance's hellhound wouldn't rest.

Fleance had a horrible feeling he knew what he needed to do.

His hellhound wanted to hunt. And Parker was the prey it had been seeking all along.

*

A week later, Rhys and Manu caught him sneaking out of town.

It was midnight. The air was cool and fresh, heavy with summer, the moonlight just enough for Fleance to see by. He was walking through the forest, a pack on his back and his passport burning a hole in his pocket.

The other hellhounds slipped out from between the trees like wraiths. Manu, so tall and broad-shouldered he looked more like a bear shifter than a hound, and Rhys, who somehow managed to still look half-transparent even when he'd shed his hellhound invisibility. Except for—

"What the hell is that?" Fleance barked, wheeling around.

Rhys fidgeted with the heavy collar around his neck. "An experiment."

"What sort of experiment requires a shock collar?" Fleance's hellhound snarled inside him, teeth bared. His eyes blazed with hellfire. Even Parker had never—

"Hey, easy, easy. Hold your horses." Manu stepped between them, hands raised palms-out. "Genius here wanted to see if he could make his hellhound replicate your symptoms. The collar—I can't believe I'm the one saying this. Rhys, you tell him, it's your bloody idea."

Rhys cleared his throat. "It's a failsafe. Since Caine isn't here, if I lose control, I'll need something to stop my hellhound."

"Your hellhound could phase right through that!" Fleance retorted.

Behind Rhys, Manu groaned and mouthed *That's what I told him!* Rhys pursed his lips. "I was working on the hypothesis that if I didn't actively acknowledge that fact, my hellhound wouldn't think to do it."

"And you thought that would work?" Fleance's jaw hurt. If he'd known his packmates would pull something like this, he never would have told them about his hellhound's problems.

Rhys's eyes glinted in the moonlight, behind his thick glasses. "We're all experienced at controlling what we let ourselves think," he remarked lightly.

Fleance grimaced. He couldn't argue with that. When they'd been under Parker's control, the alpha had raked through their thoughts like leaves. "And you waited for Caine and Meaghan to be out of town before you started your little experiment?"

"It's not like I'm breaking any rules. You'd have let me know if I was," Rhys drawled. "Since I'm not a torn heap of bloody pieces on the ground, I assume I'm morally in the clear. Anyway, you're the one running away."

"He's got you there," Manu pointed out.

"I'm not—" Fleance groaned, exasperated. "Caine will understand."

"When he finds out? Which means you haven't told him. And you haven't torn yourself into tiny pieces, either, so we have to assume you're as morally in the clear as I am." Rhys grinned, his smile as narrow and sharp as his face. "Did you leave a note on your pillow? That's traditional, isn't it, when you're running away from home?"

Fleance turned away. "I don't have time for this."

"You're going after him, aren't you?" Rhys didn't need to say who he was talking about.

Fleance paused. Manu's psychic voice brushed against his mind. *He's the reason your hellhound keeps going psycho-cop.*

I couldn't replicate the symptoms. But I never fought Parker as hard as you did. My hellhound must not have been affected in the same way... Rhys pulled out a notebook and jotted something down in it. Fleance tensed automatically.

Rhys had been trying to find a way out of Parker's power ever since their former alpha first turned him. He'd been convinced there was a logical basis to their hellhound magic. Parker had taken great pleasure in disproving more than one of his theories.

Parker isn't here now, Fleance reminded himself. *He's not going to find Rhys's notes and use them on us. That's why I'm doing this, remember?*

He nodded to the notebook. "What do you mean, you never fought? You were always trying to find a way out."

"A way out of being a hellhound. Not a way out of Parker's master plan. I wanted to be out; you wanted to be *good*."

Fleance glared at him. Inside him, his hellhound seethed. Years of frustration and helplessness had crushed it down, and now he was free and had done nothing to fix the misery his former alpha had caused.

No wonder his hellhound snapped at the smallest misdeed. As far as it was concerned, Fleance had forgotten the one thing he'd always sworn to do. Make Parker pay.

"Parker is a loose end," he said out loud.

"And you're going to snip him off?" Rhys raised one eyebrow. "Do you even know where he is?"

Fleance looked past him to Manu, who looked uncharacteristically beaten-down. He acknowledged Fleance's silent question with a brief nod. "That was what I was for, wasn't it? He wanted a bolt-hole to run to if everything went wrong." His mouth twisted. "And someone to play the native guide. Flea, I can't go back there. My family doesn't know what happened to me. I can't... not like this."

"I'm not asking you to. I'm doing this alone."

Manu looked equal parts relieved and ashamed. Rhys shot him a dark look, then turned back to Fleance. "You're sure about this?"

"I've got a passport. Parker made sure of that."

"I don't mean the technicalities."

"I know." Fleance set his shoulders. "I have to do this. It's not just my hellhound, it's all of us. I meant it when I said Parker was a loose end." He didn't want to talk about this—years under Parker's thumb had taught him never to admit to anything—but he didn't want Rhys to suddenly decide to experiment with heroism. "You can't still feel him in your mind, can you?"

"Of course not." Rhys flicked through his notebook. "My current theory is the former pack bonds are severed entirely after an alpha takeover. I wonder if the same is true of other shifter bonds. I—" He broke off and his eyes narrowed. "Wait. Can *you* still sense him?"

Fleance nodded slowly. The other two shifters paled and took a half-step backwards. He didn't blame them.

Parker wasn't part of the constellation that was his pack. He was a darker patch in the darkness beyond the stars—disconnected, but waiting.

"None of us knows how this is meant to work," he said. "But having Parker in my head still feels wrong. I won't feel like the pack's safe until he's gone, and I don't want to involve Caine and Meaghan. Not with the babies so close."

The other two nodded. The certainty of their understanding was almost enough to drive the guilt from his heart. They said their goodbyes, with Manu and Rhys promising to defray their alpha's reactions to discovering he was gone, and he headed down towards the road.

Fleance had been turned years before either of them, but Manu and Rhys had been his allies under Parker's thumb and now they were the closest thing he had to family. He already missed the close camaraderie of the pack.

A few days later, stepping onto a plane that would take him to Manu's home country of New Zealand, the constellation in his head became harder and harder to concentrate on. Physical distance had its similarities to psychic distance—he already knew that his telepathic voice had limits, but the discovery that putting hundreds of miles between him and the rest of the pack made their connection feel more distant rocked him. Especially when he was halfway over the South Atlantic and the Parker-shaped darkness in his mind was joined by a new feeling: something that pulled him forward, tugging at his soul as hard as he was trying to keep hold of his pack sense.

He closed his eyes. This had to mean he was going in the right direction, he told himself. He just had to get through the flight, and through finding Parker and whatever happened next, and then he could go home.

Back to the closest thing he had to a real family.

2

SHEENA

S heena Mackay could not wait to get away from her family.

Okay, sure, she was far enough away from them right now that she couldn't feel their telepathic voices knocking relentlessly at the walls she'd had to put up around her mind, but that wasn't good enough. Her phone had been buzzing since she woke up. It had kept buzzing as she said goodbye to the cousins she'd been staying with in Wellington—*seriously*, if her folks wanted to check in with her, couldn't they just call *them*? Get the gossip without bothering her?—and now, in the middle of the Desert Road halfway up the North Island of New Zealand, it was *still buzzing.*

How did she even have reception out here?

She shook out her dark curls and sat back, trying to coax a sliver of comfort from the bus seat. But there was not even a sliver to be found. Generations of butts had sat in that seat before her, she reckoned, and each of them had squashed a wee bit more puff out of the seat cushion until there was none left for her.

Her phone buzzed again, and she checked it. Finally—the one member of her family she could count on not to ask her if she was *sure* she felt up to traveling on her own, and had she packed enough snacks in case she got hungry, and how no one would blame her if she wanted to put off the trip for a few weeks or months so that Cousin This or Auntie That could come with her, or ideally wrap her in bubble wrap and lock her in her room so she couldn't get herself into any dangerous situations...

She plugged in her earbuds, accepted the video call and propped the phone against the back of the seat in front of her.

Her cousin Aroha's face appeared on-screen. Aroha was a few months older than Sheena's barely scraping twenty-three, with long dark hair and a wicked smile. Her voice crackled through Sheena's earbuds.

"Have you not even left the country yet? Geez, cuz, get a move on."

Sheena laughed. "I'm trying!" She lifted her phone so that her cousin Aroha could see out the bus window. "Guess where I am."

"Move your thumb off the camera then, egg."

"Fussy much..." Sheena held the phone up in front of her face, careful of her fingers, so she could see the same landscape she was showing to her cousin. Aroha was half the country away, back in the South Island, while Sheena bussed her way north. That was weird to think about. They'd grown up together—or failed to grow up, their parents might say—school, uni, work. And now Sheena was heading off to see the world and Aroha was staying home.

Stop it, she told herself firmly. Her inner sheep twitched its nose. *No, not you. Me! I have to stop acting like they're all right about me and I'm just some silly lamb who can't cope on her own.*

"Is that Ngauruhoe?" Aroha sounded awed.

"Yeah."

The mountain stood proudly on the rolling plains, cloaked in snow. Seeing it like this, Sheena could see where the stories of Ngauruhoe and the other North Island mountains warring their way across the landscape had come from. The mountain looked as though it might rear up at any moment.

"Nice." Aroha poked a finger accusingly at the camera; Sheena could just see her, reflected in the window. "But it's not exactly Las Vegas, is it?"

"I'm trying! Gotta do Roto-Vegas first, see the fam up there." Rotorua. Sulfur City. She'd only been there once before, on a family road trip when she was ten. *Old enough to keep herself out of trouble but not so old she goes looking for it,* Nana had said, which was wishful thinking. Sheena never had any trouble finding trouble. Her sheep made sure of that.

She caught her own eyes in her reflection and winced. Last time she'd been in Rotorua, thanks to her sheep's blithe absent-mindedness, she'd wandered into a cordoned-off zone and found herself at the edge of a sinkhole bubbling with mud. Her sheep had pulled its head out of the clouds long enough to panic, she'd shifted... and front-page news on the local paper the next day had been the story of the plucky fire-service cadet who'd rescued a miniature lamb from a sizzling mud bath.

Sheena's mum still had the photo on her mantelpiece.

"I can't believe they're making you visit all the rellies before you go on your OE," Aroha said.

Sheena turned the phone around so that she could see her cousin properly. It gave her time to bite back her automatic response: *I can't believe you're not coming with me.*

The 'Big OE', or Overseas Experience, was a rite of passage for young New Zealanders. Pretty much everyone Sheena had been at school with had, facing a life cooped up on a tiny island at the bottom of the world, instead springboarded themselves as far overseas as they could manage to spend their early twenties bartending or waiting tables in the UK and the USA. Sheena was a little late off the mark, but she'd finally scraped together enough money for a plane ticket to the USA and a buffer to live off while she looked for work. Her visa had come through the month before, her flight was booked for a few days in the future, and the next stage of her life was so close she could almost taste it.

"I can't believe I'm actually going," she said instead. "Everyone's acting like I'm going to get myself murdered the moment I step off the plane."

"Just don't absent-mindedly wander into any trouble. That shouldn't be hard, right?"

"Har, har." Sheena sighed. "Seriously. And now I'm visiting all the rellies before I go... I feel like Mum arranged that just so I'd feel bad about leaving and change my mind. It's having the opposite effect though." She made a face. "Everyone keeps saying how much I've *grown*."

"They're just trying to make you feel better."

"What, about being bigger than I was when I was pre-pubescent?"

"All I'm saying is people saying that last time they saw you, you were knee-high to a grasshopper, doesn't mean much when you're now only waist-high."

"Hey! You're just jealous because I won more A&P shows than you."

"I think you'll find it's my name on the rosettes, ya manus." Aroha did the finger at the camera and laughed.

"Your name and my codename." The Agricultural and Pastoral show had been a key date on the calendar in the small town where they grew up. Local kids raised up sheep or calves during the spring and competed at the festival to see who'd produced the biggest and best-trained animal. Sheena had never won biggest... or most obedient... but she had a pinboard full of 'Cutest Lamb' rosettes at her parents' house.

"Whatever, Tinkerbell. And—come on. You must be used to everyone worrying by now."

"Yeah..." She was used to it, and she *got* it. Really. She'd been born premature, and her inner sheep had never grown larger than lamb-sized. She still had dodgy lungs. But being small didn't mean she was totally pathetic. She wasn't going to let it stop her going on her OE. In fact, it made the trip all the more tempting. She had months of freedom ahead of her, a chance to do all the fun stuff she could never do at home, surrounded by cousins and aunts and uncles.

All the fun stuff.

"From the look on your face right now maybe we *should* all be worried," Aroha deadpanned. "But you know why you're doing the family rounds, though, right? They all think you're going to meet your mate and be too busy fucking happily ever after to come back."

"Aroha!"

It felt like everyone in the bus turned to look at her. Sheena slunk down in her seat, mouthing an apology. Her cheeks burned, even though she knew the other passengers were only staring at her because she'd squeaked her cousin's name so loudly she drowned out the music blaring from the seat across the aisle. She was wearing earbuds. No one else had heard what Aroha said.

"Why're you looking at me like that? It's true."

"That's..." *You can't be serious*, Sheena was about to say. Except she was the only one protesting. Her sheep thought Aroha was being perfectly reasonable.

Like you could recognize 'reasonable' if it danced naked in front of you, Sheena huffed at it.

Well... her sheep replied, dozily. *I don't think 'reasonable' would be naked? Though that would be nice.*

That's not the point!

Sheena rubbed her forehead and turned her focus back to Aroha. Her cousin was sitting up in bed, her back against the wall. Thank God. If Aroha had come out with something like that in front of the rest of the family, Sheena probably would have disappeared in a blaze of embarrassment.

Which would be standard operating procedure for Aroha. But she hadn't teased Sheena about it at her goodbye party, where it would have had maximum results. She'd waited until they were talking in private.

Relatively private, Sheena amended, glancing at the full bus around her. The woman in the seat next to her gave her a tired look that said, as clearly as if she'd spoken aloud, *Please don't make any more noise.*

Sheena did her best apologetic grimace and turned back to her phone.

Wait.

Aroha had just dropped a perfect bombshell like that, and *hadn't* immediately followed it up? She was the queen of the one-two hit, not the one-hit-and-give-you-time-to-recover.

Sheena frowned. Aroha wasn't even *looking* at her. Her eyes were fixed on something offscreen with an intensity that Sheena suspected meant she wasn't looking *at* anything at all. Just looking away. If that wasn't enough, she started twisting a strand of her hair so hard Sheena was worried she would yank all the strands right out.

"Oh!" Sheena gasped, so startled by the realization that she had to fight back her sheep's urge to leap up and run around the nearest paddock until whatever had surprised her had gone away. The woman next to her tutted ferociously. "Sorry!" Sheena said quickly. Her whole brain, sheep and all, was fizzing. "*That's* why you're not coming with me? Seriously?"

"I have things I want to do with my life!" Aroha protested, throwing up her hands. The video feed swooped and then resettled to show her face. She was biting her lip. "Not that finding the fated love of my life and having babies ever after isn't *doing something*, but I've got things to do here, first." Her chin went out stubbornly, an expression Sheena knew as well as the back of her own hand.

"You could have said something. I thought you just didn't want to be stuck in a plane with me for thirty hours," she joked.

"Well, yeah, that too." Aroha shot her a sly smile that dissolved too quickly. "Isn't that why you're going away, though? Don't tell me you never thought about it."

"I didn't."

"Why are you going, then?"

"To get away from you lot," she retorted automatically, but her mind was already leaping ahead, following the train of thought Aroha had shoved in front of her.

Every shifter had a soulmate somewhere in the world. Everyone knew that. It was no question the most magical part of being a shifter, because it was the only thing Sheena had ever known to break through her uncles' stoic Southern Man shells to reveal the tenderness and passion they hid deep inside. *Very* deep.

But she hadn't thought about it for herself. Finding your soulmate and settling down was part of being grown up, like buying a house and owning a matching dinner set. She'd spent so long filing it away with the other things she was definitely not going to manage anytime soon that she hadn't even considered it might actually happen to her.

Now, for the first time since she was seven years old and competing with Aroha over who could come up with the most fantastic-sounding mate, she really thought about it.

She might find her mate out there. The one person in the whole world who was perfectly suited to her. Which was a bit of a worry, really. Sheena sometimes thought *she* wasn't suited to herself, especially when something startled her sheep and the next thing she knew, she'd run off somewhere and got herself lost.

But the thing that hit her like a rugby ball to the chest was the idea that being bound to someone so inextricably might mean she never came home again.

It did happen. Aroha was right. Maybe that was why her parents had insisted she do this massive roadie and see all her relatives before she went overseas. They were worried that she would find her mate and immediately settle down wherever she was at the time, like a seed blown on the wind. Somewhere overseas, never to come home again.

She looked out at the unfamiliar landscape flashing past the windows. Sheena had grown up in Central Otago, a land of endless skies and sweeping hills that changed their color by the season—green, then gold, tussocks that moved like an ocean in the wind, parting around the jutting tors of granite that pushed up like islands. Sunlight was sharp there, slicing flat shadows into the mountains and burning your skin wherever it touched.

It was sharp here, too, but the land was different. Ngauruhoe straddled the landscape, its white cape of snow enhancing its classic volcano shape. Where the road cut through the sides of low hills it revealed rich red-brown earth, shot through with layers of black volcanic ash. A strange yearning twisted at Sheena's heart. She'd lived in New Zealand all of her twenty-three years and spent all but a handful of weeks in the South Island. What was she doing, going halfway across the world, when she hadn't even explored the country on her own doorstep?

I'm not going forever, she reminded herself. *It's just a trip.*

Unless she met her mate.

She swallowed.

Aroha was still talking. "Hey, my shift starts soon, I'd better go. Wait—shit, your mum asked me to remind you about something and I've forgotten what it was."

"Hah, and you don't even have my excuse." Sheena's voice didn't give away the worry twisting inside her.

"Shut up." Aroha groaned and smacked herself on the forehead. Sheena grinned at her.

"Do you reckon if you do that enough, you'll knock loose your inner animal?"

The woman in the next seat gave her a *very* odd look. Sheena wasn't worried that she'd revealed the secret existence of shifters—you could get away with a lot, she'd discovered, being a tiny white girl with big eyes and a tendency to squeak when startled. The woman probably thought she was talking metaphorically. Or that it was a sex thing.

She mouthed another 'Sorry' at her neighbor and tried to look like the sort of person who wouldn't be talking about a sex thing over the phone on an InterCity bus.

Aroha made a face. "Like I want some dumb animal inside me telling me what to do. Bad enough having the fam in my business all the—hah! Got it." She snapped her fingers. "Your mum asked me to tell you to find out what's happening with Auntie Fiona and Auntie Rena. Remember at Christmas, how they wouldn't shut up about that building development thing they were doing? Your mum says they've gone quiet."

"Oh, so she's sending me in to get the latest gossip?" Honestly, the idea of serving up some gossip that wasn't to do with herself sounded like a nice change.

"Mm. Last she heard, they were approached by some overseas investor. Basically I think she wants you to find out if the aunties are suddenly multi-millionaires in which case they should put some money into doing up Nana's place."

"All good," Sheena said. "I'm getting dropped there, anyway."

"Cool. Call me when you're actually overseas, okay?"

Sheena reassured her that she would, both of them knowing full well that either Aroha or one of their parents would call ten minutes before she was due to get on the plane and panic about her having left something behind, and they'd talk then. She tucked her phone into her backpack and stared out across the landscape.

She had her whole future ahead of her. One day, that would include her mate. But Aroha was right: she had so much she wanted to do before then. Like come back here and explore the volcanic landscape. Staring at it wasn't enough. She wanted to clamber over creek beds, feel the rich soil under her fingernails, chew on the tussock and heather to see if it tasted the same as back home…

I don't want to fall in another hole, her sheep bleated plaintively. Sheena snorted.

Fall in a hole and see if they're the same as the holes I fall in back home, she added to her to-do list. She grinned as her sheep bleated in frustration. *Don't worry. We won't have a chance to fall into anything. We're only here overnight, and then Fiona and Rena are driving us up to Auckland.*

No mud pits, her sheep said firmly.

That's up to you, isn't it? I'm not the one who got us into the last one.

The sun was shining through the windows. Outside, the temperature must have been in the single digits, but inside was warm and cozy. Sheena had been up early to catch the bus from Wellington, and those lost hours of sleep were tapping on her shoulder. She closed her eyes. *Just for a minute,* she told herself.

"Stop for Sheena Mackay—hey, chickie, wake up!"

Sheena jerked awake. "'s me," she garbled as the driver called her name again. "Here!" She resisted the urge to raise her hand like she was in school, and jumped up. "I'm awake—sorry, sorry…"

It wasn't completely a lie. Her sheep was instantly awake, but her human body clung to sleep like King Kong to the Empire State Building. She was halfway down the aisle when she realized she'd forgotten her pack and had to go back for it.

"Sorry!" she burst out again as she grabbed her bag and fumbled it and almost crushed the woman who'd been giving her looks the whole trip.

"Oh, for heaven's sake," the woman snapped in the exact right tone to send panic shooting through her sheep's extra-nervous system. "Just get a move on, will you!"

Sheena got a move on, sharpish. By the time the world stopped spinning and she began to wonder if her seat neighbor had some sheepdog shifter in her family tree, the bus was a distant speck and Sheena was alone on the side of the road.

The world might have stopped spinning, but her head hadn't. She bent over, hands on her knees, and waited for the blood to return to her brain.

Well done us, she thought wryly once the world felt normal again. *That was as bad as when I had Mrs. Powell for PE.*

Sorry. Her sheep sounded as baffled as it always did after something tripped its run-like-stink instincts. *I just...*

I know. You're just looking out for me. I'm just glad Fiona and Rena aren't here yet, they'd probably confiscate my passport.

Sheena brushed off her knees—it was more habit than anything else because she hadn't actually gone head-over-feet in her rush to run, this time—and looked around.

She was in the right place, at least. That was a good start. For having just been caught up in her sheep's flight-or-more-flight response, it was a *really* good start. The bus had dropped her just off South Highway 5, right in front of a billboard advertising *Silver Springs*. The sign had a picture of a serene town center on it, complete with a fountain and small children playing with a friendly dog, and a helpful note about there still being sections for sale.

And she had her backpack with her. Even better. *Ten out of ten,* Sheena told herself and her sheep.

Except her aunts weren't there. Eight out of ten.

She checked her phone and swore. No signal. And since she'd been asleep for the last how-many kilometers, she had no idea how long she'd had no signal for. It could have been hours. Fiona and Rena could have been trying to get in touch with her most of the day to tell her the plans had changed, and she wouldn't know.

Sheena let out a long, slow breath than plumed in the air. "Well I can't sit on my arse here waiting," she told the Silver Springs sign. "They might be ages. Anyway, there's only the one road…"

Hitching her backpack higher on her shoulders, she started to walk down it.

Winter in the middle of the North Island was almost as good as winter down south, she decided. The air was sharply cold, clean and fresh with the promise that whatever came next—hail, snow, sleet—would be here to stay, blanketing the land in icy sheets. And something was definitely coming: the sky had darkened while Sheena napped, and the clouds were thick overhead. Much earlier, the bus driver had reminded everyone to hire a locator beacon if they were planning to get out on any tramping tracks, but Sheena strode out into the cold with all the confidence of someone who had her own long woolen coat on standby and no desire to go farther off the main road than required to get to a warm, insulated house.

As she made her way along the freshly sealed road, the rolling paddocks gave way to thick bush. Spiky-leaved manuka and tree ferns battled with bushy titi for space—or would when spring broke later in the year. Now they rested in each other's arms like siblings who had forgotten what they were fighting about.

Sheena scowled. She wished she could forget her constant battles with her family. She loved them, but... sheesh. They just couldn't find it in themselves to see her as anything other than an under-cooked, helpless lamb. They were so determined to cotton-wool her that none of them except Aroha would even give her the satisfaction of even a good argument about it! They thought she was so *helpless.* As though just because she was smaller than them, she couldn't handle *anything.*

Bad enough being the youngest cousin, she thought, batting a low-hanging fern frond out of the way. *Being* literally *tinier than some of my cousins' kids when I'm shifted... No wonder no one takes me seriously.*

Her sheep sighed. *Remember when wee Mikey was the same size as me? He almost flattened me when he jumped on me the other day.*

Well, there's another upside to traveling by ourselves. No giant ten-year-olds tackling us to the ground. Sheena blew out a cloud of vapor and looked around.

Her breath wasn't the only cloud under the trees. White steam seeped through the branches. Sheena sniffed.

"Oh, nasty," she muttered at the smell of rotten eggs.

Silver Springs was a few kilometers out of Rotorua. Far enough she had no idea what direction the city was, close enough that the smell that made Roto-Vegas famous permeated the air. The geothermic activity around Rotorua gave it a distinct rotten-egg smell. She remembered the worst thing about it being that it wasn't a constant smell. It came in waves. Stinky, stinky waves.

The hot pools made up for it, though. Maybe. If you had a blocked nose.

But the smell and the steam told her that there might be a creek nearby. A hot-water creek, even. Maybe she could get a soak in before she headed up to Auckland. She needed one, after that bus trip. And before the next trip. And the long-haul flight…

She was five meters into the bush before she realized what she was doing. Frozen leaf litter crackled under her feet as she stumped back towards the road.

"Come *on*," she muttered at herself. "Dumbarse! Being a shifter won't help me if I fall into another sinkhole. Remember last time?"

Sorry, her sheep bleated, and Sheena sighed as she made her way back to the road.

"It's not you, it's *me*. No wonder everyone still treats me like I'm a little lamb. I never stop and think…"

Sheena wrinkled her nose. That last blast of wholesome natural air hadn't just smelled like sulfur. Her sheep wasn't great at sorting scents into more categories than 'try to eat it' and 'scary, run away', but it smelled like… smoke.

Good smoke? her sheep suggested. *Wood fire…
bonfire… nice fires?*

Could be. Could… not be.

It smelled like a *lot* of smoke. Bonfire? It'd have to
be a massive one.

Something Aunt Fiona had said last Christmas
trickled into Sheena's mind. Building around
Rotorua was a real hassle, she'd said, because even if
the ground didn't literally bubble away underneath
you, the constant sulfuric gases ate away at the
wiring.

Could something like that have happened and
caused a fire at Silver Springs?

Forget stopping and thinking. Sheena dropped her
pack and ran.

Branches whipped past her face. She made it back
to the road just as it broke out from the surrounding
bush, revealing a shallow basin in the clearing: Silver
Springs. Her brain felt like it was short-circuiting as
she stared out over the clearing and its just-finished
houses.

She'd seen the plans—they all had, that Christmas
just gone. Sheena's mum had grumbled that she
was surprised Fiona and Rena hadn't given them
all copies of the blueprints as presents. Not the
properties themselves; oh, no. Silver Springs was the
result of years and years of investments and planning.

Once the houses sold, Fiona and Rena would be set for life.

On the plans, everything had been neat and tidy. Clusters of houses—some designed to look like alpine chalets, some drawing on the classic design of good old Kiwi corrugated-iron sheds—connected by a road that wound through the basin in tandem with a picture-perfect stream. On the far side of the basin was the house that had started it all: Rena's family home, a patchwork homestead with generations of additions and add-ons. The design of the new houses had drawn from this original: the angle of the roof here, a bay window there, wood or metal cladding there. Chaotic, but beautiful. The perfect combination of Fiona's inner sheep and Rena's inner tūī.

That was on the plans. In person, it was on fire.

Sheena tried to think past *Oh God, it's all on fire*, but it was no use. Her brain kept circling back around.

It's all on fire.

She breathed out hard. When the vapor cleared, everything was still all on fire.

Which was all the opportunity her sheep needed to panic.

Run! it bleated, and off Sheena went, zig-zagging down the road to the nearest cul-de-sac like a mad rugby ball. *Not into the fire!* she shrieked at it as her legs carried her along with her sheep's mad instincts. "Not into the—*aaargh!*"

Flames roared from the nearest house. Heat slapped her face, viciously close. Shocked, her sheep let go of her body and Sheena stumbled back, not stopping until she was back on the tree line.

What is wrong with you? she asked her sheep as her chest heaved.

Someone might be trapped in there!

Sheena gritted her teeth. Maybe her relatives were right about her, after all. She couldn't be trusted to look after herself. *And you wanted to help them by getting us both burned alive? We're not fireproof, remember? Just like we're not barbed-wire-fence-proof and hole-full-of-boiling-mud-proof!*

Wool is a little bit fireproof, it muttered.

It's not—

Better than acrylic! it chirped. Actually *chirped.* Sheena groaned and buried her face in her hands.

'Better than acrylic' isn't going to help against THAT! Sheena almost choked as the breeze carried a waft of stinking smoke over to her. *Besides, who were you planning to save?*

Silver Springs was a ghost town. There weren't any cars in the driveways; no one was living here yet, were they?

Just Fiona and Rena.

Fiona and Rena, who were meant to come and pick her up. And hadn't.

Sheena's heart thudded in her throat.

FIONA! she shouted, sending her telepathic voice out like a fishing line across the basin. *RENA! ARE YOU THERE? CAN YOU HEAR ME?*

There was no response. Her fishing-line didn't catch on anyone's mind… which wasn't unusual. She always had trouble directing her telepathy towards anyone she couldn't see. It was as though her sheep's miniature-ness was reflected in all aspects of her shifter powers: her telepathic abilities, her control over her sheep when she was in human form, everything.

Sheena bit her lip so hard she tasted blood.

There was one other thing she could do before chucking herself straight into the fire. Being a sheep shifter was good for more than getting her into trouble. Aunt Fiona and her mate were part of Sheena's flock, and that meant she had other ways of sensing them.

"Ohh, I hate this I hate this I hate this," she muttered, and opened her mind.

The world in front of her eyes went fuzzy. But she didn't let herself close her eyes completely, even if she wasn't going to be using them for a few minutes. *Please let this not be a mistake,* she thought, and looked out across the fire with her psychic senses.

She was looking for other minds—other members of her flock, whose psychic presence pinged her sheep's all-clear signal—and this was always, *always* when things went wrong for her.

Opening her telepathic senses like this always made her feel so vulnerable. She never felt as small as she did when she was seeing everyone else's psychic presences laid out in front of her like a string of Christmas lights. Lambs were full of bright, bounding energy, older sheep shifters glowed like friendly hot coals, and Sheena was... small. Like a candle that could be pinched out. In her more generous moments, Sheena thought it was no wonder everyone in her family treated her like a porcelain doll. Most of the time, she was just annoyed, and kept fences up around her mind so that people couldn't see just how snuffable her flame looked and would have less reason to coo over her.

She gritted her teeth and tried not to think about that. If Fiona and Rena were around, she would be able to see them. She strained her mental eyes, hunting for any sight-feel of either of them—Fiona's wooly bonfire, Rena's warbling flutteriness. Anything.

There was nothing. Sheena sighed with relief and was busy reeling in her mind again when something moved at the far reaches of her psychic senses. She gasped. It wasn't a member of her flock, but it was *someone.* Not a light, but a presence.

Vaguely aware that the fuzzy non-psychic world was moving around her, she tried to focus her mental vision. The light pulsed gently, then flickered out.

For once, Sheena was glad to refocus on the real world and find she'd wandered off. Especially since she *hadn't* wandered into the fire. She was halfway around the tree line, arcing towards her aunts' house—exactly where she'd sensed the strange presence.

As soon as she came out of her mind's-eye blur and saw where she was, she stumbled and caught her knee on a rock, but that was par for the course.

She righted herself and ran.

Grass whipped against her shins. She half-slid, half-stumbled down onto the driveway in front of Fiona and Rena's place. She couldn't sense the mystery shifter now, but she could smell—something. Something more than the choking smoke. Something... alive.

She turned away. The fire that was consuming the rest of the township hadn't reached the homestead. Yet. Staying here a few minutes and trying to save whoever was stuck here wasn't stupid. Was it?

Or is my brain as stunted as the rest of me? Some of her cousins would probably think so. Aroha for one. Sheena swallowed.

Hello? she called, sending her telepathic voice out like a fishing line again as she reached the front door. This time, something caught it. *Hello—whoever you are, there's a fire—*

Did her aunts have a house guest? They tended to adopt anyone who crossed their path. What if they'd left their visitor here while they went to pick her up? And she'd missed them, somehow, but their guest was still here. That must have been what happened.

Break the door down! her sheep suggested.

I'm not strong enough to do that! A dozen images flashed through her mind, each less likely than the last. Or any of those things! I can't FLY, how am I meant to get in the skylight? If there even is a skylight!

She pounded on the door again and shouted out loud as well as telepathically. A quick glance over her shoulder. The fire hadn't leaped to the nearest cluster of houses yet, but it couldn't be long. "Hey! Hello?! Is anyone in there?"

Her sense of the strange shifter kept flickering in and out of focus. At last she swore and pulled out her phone. By some miracle, she had signal again. And a few percent of battery left; enough? Maybe?

She found her Aunt Fiona's contact and called her. The phone rang for long enough to get her worried, then she heard her aunt's voice.

"Sheena? How are you—oh, f—" Fiona let off a string of curses. "You were meant to arrive today.

With everything else going on—shit. Tell me you're not—"

"I'm at the house." Sheena almost shouted down the phone, not sure whether Fiona's garbled speech was a result of a bad connection or her just not listening properly.

"No, don't be at the house! Shit! Fuck, fuck, *fuck* this whole piece of shit—"

Sheena didn't have time for her aunt's favorite rhetorical devices. "Auntie Fi, I'm here, everything is on fire—"

"He really did it?" That wasn't Fiona's voice; Rena must have been close enough to the phone to hear, or Fiona had her on loudspeaker. "Get out of there, girl, fast as you can."

"I wasn't planning on sticking around," Sheena grumbled, one eye still on the fire behind her. "I just need to get your houseguest to wake the hell up first and come with me!"

"Houseguest?"

"Whoever it is you've got staying. If you could call them, or tell me where you keep the spare key and I'll let myself in and get them up—I keep trying to contact them but there's something wrong with my telepathy, I can't reach them." She thumped her fist on the door again. "Open up!"

The door swung open.

"Sheena, hon, we don't have anyone staying with us." Fiona's voice was eerily flat.

Sheena blinked into the sudden darkness behind the open door. "What do you mean? I can sense that someone's here. And... and the door's open now, actually, so I'll just..."

"Sheena, you need to get out of there. Right now. It's not—"

Her voice cut off. Sheena frowned and looked at her phone. Dead.

But the door was open. Sheena took a step forward before her aunt's words settled in. *Get out of here? Right now? It's not—what? What isn't it?*

Safe? She looked over her shoulder. Everything was very, very on fire—no shit it wasn't safe.

"Hello?" she called out tentatively, pushing the door further open. "My name's Sheena. I don't know if you've looked outside lately, but..."

There was no one inside but suddenly, Sheena's skin prickled with a wash of cold sweat. The air flickered and she jerked back, raising her hand to shield herself from... nothing?

"Wh-what?" she muttered to herself. The corridor was empty. There wasn't even a curtain over the door that could have swung across and frightened her, so why was she so shaken?

It had felt like something was coming straight at her, and then... nothing.

Sheena raised one shaking hand to push her hair off her face. She was trembling so badly her phone fell to the ground.

What's wrong? her sheep asked, nuzzling against her. *Why are you acting so weird?*

"I—" Sheena licked her lips. Her breath was coming in short gasps. *I don't know? You don't feel that?*

Feel what?

Feel... She shivered. *Afraid?*

No, her sheep replied stoutly. *I don't care what you said about being no better than acrylic. I'm not going to let some stupid fire stop us from doing what's right!*

Not afraid of the fire, of... Sheena shook herself. *Yes* of the fire, she meant. Didn't she? Because there was nothing else to be afraid of. Just fiery death.

And letting some poor arsehole die because she was too busy freaking out like the helpless munter everyone thought she was to help them.

That scared her. Letting herself down because of her limitations was one thing, but letting down other people? She couldn't live with that.

And you dropped your phone! Her sheep sounded scandalized. *I don't know where you get off, teasing me about being scatterbrained when you don't even—look, it's right there, pick it up before you stand on it or something—*

Sheena shook her head. Her sheep wasn't making any sense. She was shivering like she'd just crashed into a frozen lake, and it was talking about her *phone?* She didn't have time for this.

Her sheep was still trying to nudge her back towards her phone. She reached out as though she was going to pick it up and, while her sheep was distracted by its success, quickly constructed a mental picnic basket around it.

Hey! her sheep bleated. *Mmmf!*

There, Sheena thought. She felt dizzy for a moment, as the basket that would keep her sheep temporarily out of her hair settled in place.

The picnic basket was the one surefire method she had of stopping her sheep from running away with her. It was like an internal version of the walls she used to keep other shifters from peeking into her inner self. With the walls on the outside and the picnic basket on the inside, what was left of Sheena felt like she was being squeezed in a sliding door, but at least she wasn't constantly fighting her sheep's twitchy instinct to run at the first sign of trouble.

She hurried inside, blinking as her eyes adjusted to the darkened corridor. "Hey! If you're in here—" she began and froze.

There it was again. The uncanny sensation that something was rushing towards her. And... a smell.

The hairs on the back of her neck rose. This wasn't the normal geothermic stink, even if the way it kept wafting in and out of reach was the same. She took a few tentative steps, moving her head from side to side to try to pin it down.

It was *nasty*. Sweet, but bad sweet. Like coming back from a week away and finding the power had gone off. Milk curdled, vegetables slimy, cheese weeping. Or a glass of wine left in the sun until it was all vinegar and flies.

She grimaced, but the smell was gone again as quickly as it had appeared. Sheena lowered her head bullishly. Someone was here—someone who *shouldn't* be, obviously, given how they were avoiding her, but she couldn't let that stop her. Or a wee bit of BO. She needed to get them out of here.

"My name's Sheena," she called, then glanced back over her shoulder. The fire hadn't gotten any closer. "Look, I know shit's weird right now, but it's going to be safer outside than stuck in here—"

The words died in her throat.

In the half a second she'd looked away, the hallway in front of her had filled with smoke. Thick, rancid yellow smoke. *It's on fire*, she thought, telling herself to move, reminding her sheep that out of fright or flight it had *always* chosen running the hell away, so time to get on with that, right? Because where there was smoke there was… fire…

Two fires. Pinpricks of flame, not on the walls or the floor but floating in mid-air. They blazed brighter as Sheena watched and the sweet-sick smell filled her nostrils.

Not fires, she realized as they got closer and the smoke below them twisted into the shape of fangs. *Eyes.*

Run.

It wasn't her voice, or her sheep's. It didn't nudge up against her mind like another shifter's telepathic voice. It rattled around the inside of her skull and pressed down on her until her knees almost gave out. Icy fingers clenched around her heart.

Run!

She ran. So fast and so blindly that she almost sprinted straight into the fire. Her feet skidded as she turned around. The trees—she had to get to the trees. Away from the fire, away from—

Footsteps behind you in the darkness. A chill breath on your neck. Eyes in the shadows. There's no escape. It will find you.

Fear rose up inside Sheena, some primeval instinct that overrode everything else in her mind except the knowledge that she couldn't possibly get away. Eventually, it would find her. But even if running was useless, she had to keep running, because it was better that exhaustion got her than—than—

Not that way! her sheep screamed at her. *The fire!*

Sheena swore as heat burst against her face. A ragged breath and her lungs filled with the rotten stench she'd scented earlier. She twisted away from something she couldn't see but *knew* was there and ran down the street. *Fuck.* Into the street, surrounded by houses that were *on fire*, and—wait—there—if she could reach that gap, she'd be able to make it back into the trees—

She almost made it before another crash of fear sent her stumbling backwards.

Angry tears sprang to her eyes as she hit the ground. Gravel tore at her hands and knees. This time when she caught the sweet-sick scent, she kicked out automatically and hit—nothing.

She stood up slowly. Her face felt hot and stung when she touched it. She winced, eyes skittering over the burning houses, the smoke coiling up in the still air, the empty streets. The nothingness that frightened her so badly she'd almost run into a burning building.

Think, she begged herself silently. Not her sheep, for once. This time, she was begging herself, because she was the one whose mind wanted to run away from whatever was... whatever this was. *Just stop, and... think.*

Something was after her. Something that made every part of her remember she was prey, not predator. She couldn't see it yet, but she knew it was coming, the same way she knew up was up and down was down. Maybe that made her crazy.

She might be crazy, but she wasn't *stupid.* Not so stupid that she would run straight into a fire instead of away from it. Not unless what was happening here was *real.*

She had to do something to defend herself.

What? her sheep bleated, confused. *What are you defending yourself from?*

A sob of laughter lodged in her throat. Her sheep was right to be confused. Defend herself? She was a sheep shifter. Sheep didn't defend themselves; they panicked, and ran astray, and let themselves be herded into little boxes.

Wait… Her blood ran icy cold. Was that what had just happened to her? Was she being herded?

Herded by what? her sheep sounded baffled. *What are you doing? Stop running!*

Stop running? No, I can't let it—

Sheena blinked. Her heart was still racing, her armpits and back were wet with sweat, but she wasn't afraid anymore.

The fear had slipped away so neatly, it was as though it had never existed.

A new sliver of unease wound itself around her heart. It felt different to the fear. It felt like it was *hers,* as though the fear before had been somehow outside of herself. Battering against her defenses. *Herding* her.

She stood completely still, blood hammering in her ears. What was going on?

What is going on? her sheep repeated. *Hang on—can you smell that?*

Hard not to, she replied. The putrid, sweet rotten smell felt like a physical sludge in her nostrils.

No, not that... Her sheep's voice faded out and Sheena felt its attention turn away from what she was seeing and hearing. She clutched desperately for the picnic basket but her sheep was too quick for her. It hijacked her senses and Sheena felt dizzy as her body tried to concentrate on too many smells and sounds at the same time. When it tried to drag up her psychic vision again, she put her foot down.

This is not the time! she told it, exasperated. *Why do you always—*

Another swell of fear rose up, coiling around her like an icy wind trying to find a way in. Sheena held perfectly still. This wasn't normal. She'd been afraid before, scared, startled, but nothing like this.

She looked at the tree line and dread trickled down her spine. It was twenty meters away, maybe less. She could usually run that distance without even noticing. In fact, she generally called it a win when her sheep got less than a hundred meters before she noticed.

Run, the fear told her, and crashed down over her head like a surf wave pushing her underwater. Run back where she'd come from. Back towards the flames.

Sheena bared her teeth. This wasn't *her* fear. Something was doing this to her. And if it thought it could *herd* her, well, she'd show it exactly how good she was at not paying attention to anyone else's instructions—

Hissing laughter filled her head. Sharp fangs snapped at the back of her neck and Sheena jerked forward, her moment of bravery vanishing like mist. She twisted around and seeing nothing where she'd just felt teeth was worse than seeing those burning eyes in the dark hallway.

Because it's behind you, always behind you, don't let it catch you.

Sheena lurched forwards. Her sheep yanked at her legs, almost making her stumble, and then her foot caught on something. The ground rushed up to smack her. She flung her hands forward to break her fall and her wrist folded beneath her, but it was her ankle that twisted painfully as she went down.

Teeth gritted against the pain, she rolled onto her knees. *I know you're trying to help but just let me do this, I can't get away if we're fighting over my legs!*

What are you doing? her sheep cried out, aghast. *Don't keep running! I'm sorry about your ankle but I had to do something!*

Sheena stared at the root she'd tripped over. When her sheep had tried to take over her body, she'd stumbled directly onto it. *You did this?* Sheena screamed at it. *Are you trying to get us killed?*

You're the one trying to get us killed! You keep running towards the fire!

Because it's trying to herd me there! I know that! Pain was still shooting through her ankle and she focused on that, not her sudden panic. Her heart was beating so hard she felt like she could hardly breath past it. *How is making it so I can't get away going to help?*

Confusion throbbed in her sheep's voice. *There's nothing to get away from!*

How can you say that? Can't you feel it?

Feel what? You can't keep running into the fire! This isn't New Year's! Those are burning houses, not a bonfire! I know I got startled before and joked about being fireproof, but are you trying to get yourself killed?

Sheena's ears were buzzing. She was so terrified she could barely think straight, and now her sheep was saying it couldn't feel what she was feeling?

Why are you so scared? her sheep nuzzled against her. *There's nothing here. It's just you and me.*

But didn't you sense it? Sheena pressed her hands against her eyes. Every second she stayed here arguing with her sheep was a second she wasn't using to get away. She clambered to her feet, wincing as her ankle complained. *Didn't you see the eyes?*

The what?

Behind the door—

I didn't see anything behind the door! You stuffed me in the picnic basket! You know I can't see anything from in there!

Which had been the whole point. Sheena took a deep breath and edged along the path, wincing as she put weight on her ankle. *Something is chasing us and now I can't run! Do you want me to just lie down here and wait to die?*

What are you talking about? Nothing's chasing us! You're acting like a crazy person and that's MY job!

Her mouth went dry. Fear rolled around her, a solid force pushing her to her knees. *Can't you feel that?* Sheena almost sobbed.

And then it was gone.

Sheena ran her hands down her face. Gone, yes, but for how long? It was like a light-switch in her brain. Terror, then nothing to show for it except her shaking breaths and sweaty hands. Not that she could see anything even when she was afraid. Except for those eyes.

If they were even real. Sheena swallowed. Her sheep hadn't seen the eyes, and it hadn't felt what she felt. What if she really was losing it?

Maybe everyone is right. Her heart sank. *I can't cope alone. If I can't even trust my own eyes…*

Now I don't want you to be upset, her sheep said nervously.

Too bloody late for that. Sheena sat back.

But I think we should get up.

The fire. I know. Wouldn't that just be perfect. Run around like a fucking lunatic and then just sit here and let the fire roll straight over her. Totally in-character. No one would be surprised.

Well, yes, the fire, her sheep said gently. *But also… I told you I could smell something before, didn't I?*

When you took over my eyes and ears so I couldn't see my way out of here? Sheena felt suddenly exhausted. So what if she burned to death? It seemed inevitable now. She should just lie down right here and prove all her family right.

Yes. Promise you won't be mad?

Sheena took a deep breath. *Why would I be—*

A new scent flooded through her. Not the sweet-sick stench from before, or the throat-scorching smell of burning buildings. Something clean and masculine that filled her senses.

Sheena opened her eyes and looked in the direction her sheep was pushing her.

"Oh," she tried to say, but her whole body was paralyzed by shock and it came out more like "Oaaargh."

There was a man standing on the road, surrounded by burning buildings. Even through the smoke and heat-shimmer she could see that he was tall and leanly muscled. His black leather jacket and dark glasses made his pale skin and red hair all the more striking. She couldn't see his eyes behind the mirrored lenses of his sunglasses, but that didn't matter. He was the whole deal. Everything. So much *muchness* her mind stuttered over it.

Don't be mad, her sheep repeated, and Sheena's mouth dropped open.

I'm not mad, she told it. *I mean, I might have gone crazy, but I'm not angry.*

Oh, good! Her sheep's relief was so intense Sheena felt drunk. Or maybe she would have felt drunk anyway. Here was something that made sense. Forget the strange fear, forget jumping at shadows that Sheena-the-human couldn't explain and her sheep couldn't even sense, here was something that they both understood bone-deep.

This man was her mate.

He looked as stunned as she felt—for a moment. Before Sheena could even think about what she could say, let alone twist her tongue around the words, he walked towards her, moving with the casual grace of someone who never tripped over their own feet.

She felt dizzy, as though she was standing on the edge of a cliff. Which she was. Metaphorically speaking. Her life was splitting off into *before* and *after* and she was teetering on the edge of *after*. This was it. *He* was it. This gorgeous stranger whose hair caught the light like a live flame.

She didn't wait for him to reach her. For one glorious moment, she didn't even care that she was losing her mind and covered in soot and had probably singed her eyebrows off. Her sheep skipped like a lamb as she half-ran, half-stumbled to meet him.

He stopped in front of her and reached out with one hand, as though he wasn't sure she was real.

"Are you all right?" he asked.

His voice was like sunlight on her skin. She swallowed, opened her mouth, and absolutely failed to make any words come out. "Hngk?" she managed.

"You're hurt." His eyebrows came together above his sunglasses and he hesitated with his hand almost touching her face. "What happened h—"

He didn't get any further because Sheena threw herself into his arms and kissed him.

It should have been awkward. She barely came up to his collarbone and she'd just lunged at him with no warning but somehow it worked. His arms folded around her like she belonged in them. She wrapped her arms around his shoulders and pressed her lips against his and, God, he tasted like running wild felt, like tall grass brushing her sides and the sky wide and open above. He kissed her back, tentative until her tongue brushed against his and then he was all hunger.

Sheena's heart felt like it was going to break out of her chest. The shadowy mental paddock where her sheep spent most of its time filled with light and that light spilled out to fill every part of her. It sang through her veins from her heart to the very tips of her fingers, flaring like the sun.

Magic. Of course, just being a shifter was magic, but it was normal magic. She'd been a shifter all her life. She'd never known anything like this. It felt like she had swallowed the sun and the only thing holding it in was the mental fence she had built in her mind.

Her skin sang where her mate touched it. Her lips tingled with excitement. She felt more alive than she ever had done. For the first time, she wasn't too small or too weak or too adorable to be taken seriously—she was just herself and herself was enough. If she'd had any doubts about that then the possessive way her mate was crushing her against his chest would have banished them instantly.

So, what the hell did she need those walls inside her mind for? The ones she used to keep everyone out. Right now, they were keeping all that light in, and…

This man was everything she wanted, and she wanted *all* of him.

She let down her defenses and the light filling her veins poured into him.

3

FLEANCE

He should have said something.

And then he couldn't say anything, because her lips were pressed against his with a wild intensity that drove all the words from his mind. There was only her, this woman he knew nothing about but knew in his soul he was meant to be with.

His mate.

Her fingers tangled in his hair, pulling him down to her height. He wrapped himself around her, her shudder of breath as their bodies pressed close echoing in his own chest. Her scent overwhelmed him, clover honey and spring blossoms, the promise of long afternoons and longer evenings. Was she a shifter? The moment the question appeared in his mind he knew the answer. Of course she was. He could sense it, a hint of her inner animal twined around everything else he could feel about her. Just as his hellhound was a part of everything that made him who he was, even if it had taken him this long to realize it. He wasn't a man with a hellhound tacked on, he was a hellhound shifter, *whole*, and thank God he was because that wholeness made him hers.

He cupped her face in his hands and kissed her with all his heart. Something unspooled deep in his chest in the shadows where his hellhound lurked, but it wasn't a shadow; it was light, gleaming so brightly gold it put the sun to shame. It unfurled like a shoot pushing through the snow, one leaf then two then enough to spread through his veins until it found the same golden light in her lips, in her fingertips pressed against his skin, in the softness of her cheek and the determined line of her jaw beneath his palms. Her heart and his, bound together.

He gasped. Their lips parted, but the spell didn't break. The shining light from the deepest part of his soul was still alight, a golden rope that connected him to the woman in his arms.

"Oh, wow," she breathed, her eyelids fluttering. Her breath hitched, and emotions shimmered down the golden rope: wonder, confusion, a shiver of embarrassment. "I, uh. I didn't expect *that* to happen so fast."

That? Fleance was confused. He'd known he was her mate the moment he saw her; wasn't that the way it was meant to work?

The golden light connecting them thrummed like a plucked guitar string. "Oh," Fleance said out loud. *That.*

The golden rope. A bond. The mate bond.

"Also, have to admit I thought it would be more, uh, metaphorical?" The mate bond twanged again. She laughed, delight burbling out of her like water from a fountain. "Holy… wow."

Her eyes focused on his. They were as bright as her voice, her laughter, the light that connected them. Flecks of gold sparkled in warm brown, like slices of sunlight cutting through the canopy to dance on the forest floor.

"I'm Sheena," she said.

"Flea—Fleance." He caught himself just in time and gave his full name, not the embarrassing nickname.

She smiled. "Hi."

"Hi."

There was more he should be saying. He knew that the same way he vaguely remembered there was something he should have said earlier, before the kiss that broke his world into *before her* and the rest of his life.

The smoke… his hellhound whispered. Fleance could have hit himself. He was standing around like a stunned fish while buildings burned all around him—and his mate. He had to get her out of here.

"I can't believe this is happening." Sheena pulled her hands away from his shoulders but kept them resting on his chest, as though she couldn't bear to stop touching him. He understood. He didn't want to lose her touch, either, the way her waist molded to his hand, the punch-drunk wonder of her body so close to his. "I thought my sheep had really lost it this time. Or I had. I thought I saw…" She shook her head. "But my sheep said there wasn't anything. I must have breathed in too much smoke." She half-smiled, as though she was trying to convince herself.

He wanted to get lost in her eyes, the tentative quirk at the corner of her lips, the almost tangible need to think that everything was fine, everything was normal, no problems here.

No. What he wanted didn't matter. What his hellhound wanted didn't matter now, either. What mattered was that he had chased the shadows in his mind to this remote, abandoned community, and although Parker's signature was clear in the burning buildings, he couldn't sense the other hellhound anywhere. No scent or sound or sight of the man who'd once controlled his life. And nothing supernatural, either. No ghost of the old chain around his soul, dragging him back.

And his mate had just said—

"You thought you saw something?" A trickle of foreboding made its way down Fleance's spine.

"It—" She shrugged, and even without the mate bond he could have seen her thoughts on her face:

No, that's crazy, it can't have happened, there's nothing wrong...

The hairs on the backs of his arms rose. Inside him, his hellhound jumped to high alert.

"We need to get out of here." He wrapped one arm protectively around Sheena and hurried back up the road towards the least on-fire part of the subdivision. *What did you see?*

Nothing.

Fleance clenched his jaw. The word had arrived in his head accompanied by a tremble of fear.

He hadn't been able to sense Parker. He'd been *glad* not to feel any remnant of the control the man once had over him. It had put one of his fears to rest: that Parker would still somehow be able to control him, despite the fact that Caine had taken over the pack.

He'd been a fool. Without the pack sense, Parker could make himself as untraceable to Fleance as he was to any other human or shifter. How could he protect anyone from a threat he couldn't even sense?

The same way the people I hurt couldn't do anything against me.

Sheena stiffened in his arms and for one horrible moment, he thought he'd let his thoughts reach her mind. Then he saw her attention wasn't on him.

"The motorway's back that way," she said, pointing behind them.

"I took a—I won't call it a shortcut," he said. "My car's this way."

"Sweet. Wait, my phone—" She looked up towards the patchwork house that overlooked the rest of the community and fear flickered across her face. It was only momentary, and as quick as it had appeared it vanished, replaced by a strangely frantic determination.

Or not so strange. Fleance tightened his arm around her.

"I left my phone at the house," she said. Her voice was normal, but the mate bond screamed like a steel cable under pressure. "I should—"

"We're getting out of here," he reminded her.

"Without calling the fire brigade?"

He recognized her sudden stubbornness. When nothing else made sense, cling to the things that did. Fewer people called on emergency services than you might expect, when under attack by hellhounds, and those that did found that human cops and firefighters were less help than they might have hoped.

Hope. It was hope that was behind the stubbornness, the need to believe that everything was going to go back to normal. And much as he wished it didn't have to be so, hope was a luxury he couldn't let his mate be fooled by.

"The fire service can't help with this," he began, and Sheena spun out of his arms.

"What are you talking about? It's in the name. *Fire.* Which there's a shit ton of here, if you hadn't noticed!"

"It's not the most dangerous thing here." She raised her chin, defiance on every inch of her face, as he bulled onwards. "You know it's true. You sensed something else, didn't you? Something you won't let yourself believe is real."

Uncertainty cracked the edge of her expression. "N-no…"

Her face was wearing the same tense mask Fleance had seen on so many other people before. Adrift in uncertainty, she was searching for something, *anything,* to cling to. She'd mistrust the proof of her own eyes and ears to convince herself that everything was fine.

That's what hellhound magic did best.

His hellhound rose up inside him. Parker *was* here. Which meant Sheena wasn't safe. He'd only met her a handful of minutes ago and he was already failing at keeping her from harm.

His hellhound snarled. *I won't let him hurt her!*

At last, Fleance thought. A good use for his hellhound's frustrated rage. He let its fire build inside him, a fierce heat next to the shining light of his connection to Sheena.

He would get Sheena out of here. Then he'd come back and find Parker, and—

Suddenly, Sheena jerked away from him, her eyes wide.

She raised one hand and pointed at his face. "Your eyes," she began, horror dawning in her own eyes. "There's smoke coming out from your glasses. I thought I was imagining things before. But you're—you're—"

Fleance stilled. He'd been too careless, let his hellhound get too close to the surface. As Sheena pointed at him accusingly, he felt smoke coiling out from behind his sunglasses.

He swallowed. "You have to trust me—"

"Oh, sure, I trust you." The sudden tightness around her eyes told him that was a lie, and his chest twisted. "Is this some kind of sick joke? That was you back in the house, wasn't it?"

He grasped for the mate bond and Sheena took another horrified step backward. The shining light splintered in his grip and he let go as the world swooped around him.

"It's not what you think," he began. "Please. Trust me." He pulled off his sunglasses and reached out to her mind again, trying to imbue his own telepathic voice with how important it was she believe him while keeping back how afraid he was.

I'll explain everything, but there isn't time—

He stopped. A wall had come down between his mind and Sheena's, impenetrable as stone. Even the golden thread connecting his heart to hers pulled tight, as though a huge weight had slammed down on it.

Splintered. Crushed. Fear dug into his heart. How much more damage could it take?

That first touch of her mind to his had been like the lick of a cool breeze. He wanted to feel it again. To roll around in it, luxuriate in the sudden mind-to-mind intimacy. He'd been able to speak telepathically to shifters ever since Parker turned him, but this was different. This, for the first time since he'd become a shifter, had felt like it was what he was meant for.

And now it was going up in smoke.

"Your eyes are on *fire*." Sheena stepped back, her jaw tightening. "That's what I saw in my aunts' house. What's going on here? Who are you?" Her fists clenched. "Did you do this? Fiona told me to leave before *he* did something. And you're—you're—"

My mate, she mouthed, as though she couldn't bear to say the words out loud. Before Fleance could say anything, she shook herself.

"No. The fear was a trick. This is a trick, too, isn't it? You're doing something to my mind. You're not really… no."

Her face had been full of fear and disgust but now, as she said that the connection between them might not be real, they melted away and were replaced by hope.

Hope that he wasn't her mate.

Blackness swirled at the edges of Fleance's vision. Not his hellhound: it was desperately silent, as though if it stayed still enough, it could take back the last thirty seconds and not ruin the one good thing in his life.

"Sheena, I—" he began, his voice ragged.

The hairs on the back of his neck rising was all the warning Fleance got that it was too late.

Don't let me ruin the moment. The voice clawed into Fleance's mind, bitter sharp and horribly familiar. *No more than you've already ruined it yourself, little Flea.*

The air behind Sheena shimmered and a hellhound stepped out of nothingness onto the empty road.

Sheena swore and reeled back towards Fleance. *Protect her!* his hellhound snarled. Fleance didn't need telling. He moved in front of her automatically, adrenaline flooding his system.

And Sheena's voice burst into his mind, jagged-edged and sharp as the light that flared between them once again.

What the fuck is that? she gasped. Emotions flooded through the mate bond: shock, confusion. Guilt. *His eyes—wait. And his smell. It wasn't you at my aunts' house, it was him.*

Fleance reached behind himself without looking and grabbed her hand. *Don't worry. I'll protect you.*

What is that?

Fleance gritted his jaw. *A hellhound. Like me.*

Angus Parker's hellhound form was the size of a small pony. In the dark, from a distance, it might look like a real dog. If you made that mistake, as Fleance knew, you were already done for. If it got close enough for you to see the acrid smoke boiling out from under its black coat, or the pits of hellfire where its eyes could be, there was no escape.

The last time he had seen Angus Parker, Caine had just made him bare his throat in surrender. Caine had fought Parker in hellhound form: the two alphas were matched for size and strength, and since Caine was an alpha, he'd been able to break the other alpha's power over him and take control of the pack.

Fleance had never seen Parker so angry. His hellhound form had melted away, but its rage had festered so close to the surface Fleance could feel it, even as he was led away in handcuffs. Now it was as though the rot had seeped through the hellhound's skin. Parker's coat was ragged and patchy, and the smoke that oozed through it was thick and greasy. Fleance felt nauseous.

It's hellhound magic, he told himself as his heartbeat thundered in his ears and a million years of evolutionary instinct told him to run. *That's all. He's just trying to frighten you.*

His own hellhound was cowering low inside him, ears flat to its skull, teeth bared. Fleance's breath locked in his throat.

Parker wasn't just trying to frighten him. He was succeeding, sending terror rolling to the very depths of his soul. And not just because of his magic.

Because Fleance, and his hellhound, knew what he was capable of.

All the more reason not to let fear distract us, he thought, as much to himself as his hellhound and convincing neither of them.

Parker's hellfire eyes trailed over him, down to his hand clenched tight around Sheena's. A rough chuckle that made the hairs on the back of Fleance's neck stand up grated out of its throat.

Patched up your lovers' quarrel already? Never say I never did anything for you, kiddo, Parker rasped.

Fleance felt sick. The idea of his uncle having anything to do with his relationship with his mate made his stomach turn.

"Yeah, okay, that's definitely what I saw," Sheena whispered from behind him, her voice thin with fright. "I take it back. Your fiery eyes are much nicer than that thing's."

The monstrous hound peeled its lips back over its fangs. *And everyone keeps saying this is a first-world* *country,** it snarled pleasantly. *I'll forgive you that 'thing' this once, sweetheart. In the future, you'll call me 'sir.'*

Sheena bristled. Fleance squeezed her hand. "She won't say anything to you in the future, because we're leaving. Now." Fleance's hellhound, even paralyzed with fear, lent its growl to his voice. He faced Parker down.

His car was two miles away, maybe more, beyond the small forest that surrounded the burning neighborhood. Behind Parker.

He had to get to it and get Sheena to safety. No matter what it took.

Parker lowered his head with a wolfish grin, as though he'd heard Fleance's thoughts. *Impossible*, Fleance reminded himself.

Leaving so soon? He could imagine how this would go if Parker was in human form: the wide smile, the friendly clap on the shoulder that turned into a grip so solid there was no escaping it. The hellhound's bare-fanged grin was a terrifying parody of Parker's gleaming salesman smile. *I'm disappointed, Flea. I'm sure you didn't come all this way to turn tail the moment you saw me. Not after all this time.*

"You don't know anything about why I'm here." He knew that was the truth. If he couldn't sense Parker's presence when he was invisible—if the alpha bond was truly broken—then Parker couldn't read his mind.

Give a man a chance, Flea. Let's see if I can guess what brought you all this way. A strange shiver rippled through the hellhound's filthy coat.

You know this guy? Sheena's voice filtered into Fleance's mind. A whisper, directed at him alone. A thin echo of the intimacy of that first kiss—but it was something. Fleance clung to it like a lifeline.

He's dangerous, he sent back, and his hellhound shuddered with relief when he felt his voice slip through a crack in Sheena's mental defenses.

Yeah? No shit. Look at him. She moved to his side, staring wide-eyed at the leering hellhound. *What do we do?*

Fleance's stomach tightened. Look at him. She was right, anyone could see the creature in front of them was a monster. And that monster had made Fleance in his image.

Shouldn't have come here, his hellhound whined. Not ready. Not strong enough.

Fleance gritted his jaw. We're here now, he reminded it. We have to be ready. Sheena needs us. And... look around you. Past the smoke. Snowy mountains, frozen trees—it's time for another Christmas miracle.

My car's at the end of a gravel road a few miles away, he said to Sheena. *Keys in my back pocket. When I say go, take them and—*

Sheena was already saying *Okay, cool, how long's a mile in real time though* when Parker growled impatiently. She froze, fingers just brushing Fleance's back pocket.

Oh, no, please, keep talking among yourselves. I can see I'm expected to hold up this whole conversation by myself. His eyes blazed. *Now, where were we? Right, right, your reasons for being here.*

"Don't matter, because we're leaving."

Damn, Flea, did I teach you that badly? The monster laughed. *No, no, you're playing it all wrong. I know something brought you here. Excuse me. Someone. And it's obvious you and the little lady didn't know each other before today. There's only one other person here.* His grin widened. *What were you thinking, Flea? You wanted to take me on?*

Keys, Fleance muttered urgently to Sheena. They didn't make a noise as she snuck them from his pocket.

Smoke hissed from Parker's nostrils. *But suddenly, whatever it was that brought you here is no longer your priority.* His huge head twisted to look at Sheena and Fleance shifted.

Now! he called as his hellhound rose up. It didn't hesitate. Whatever fear had kept his hellhound paralyzed while Parker was talking dissolved as it took form. Its massive paws hit the ground running and he lunged at his former alpha.

Too late. Parker was already moving. He writhed like a snake, dodging Fleance's attack and reaching for Sheena with one massive, claw-tipped foreclaw.

Pain ripped down the golden cord that bound Fleance to his mate. He tried to turn in mid-air and landed clumsily.

Sheena was face-down on the ground. Fleance's hellhound snarled and ran to her, pressing its snout against her shoulder.

"'m fine," she muttered. Her fingers tangled in his mane as she pulled herself up. "I—*sss*. Landed on my bad knee." She hissed with pain and struggled upright. "Can't even *dodge* without..." she began, then looked past him. The jolt of her shock in his chest was all the warning he got.

The other hellhound struck him in the flank. Fleance flew through the air. He hit the ground and sprang up against at once, leaping towards Parker before he could get to Sheena again.

Run! he yelled to his mate, and then there was no time to say or think anything. Fighting against Parker was like running along a knife's edge. One slip, one mistake, and Parker wouldn't hesitate to tear him to pieces.

Old scars pulled and twisted as he avoided Parker's teeth. Muscles he hadn't used in over a year burned. Running through Pine Valley's forests was nothing like this.

He had to get Parker away from his mate. Fleance gave up ground, letting the other hellhound drive him into the nearest burning building. Hellhounds could phase through solid matter, but they couldn't *see* through it. If he kept Parker occupied in the flames and collapsing timber, Sheena would have a chance to get away.

Parker's teeth snapped together less than an inch from his shoulder. Before he could get his balance back, Fleance spun around.

He knew what he had to do. He'd seen Parker do it. Take advantage of his opponent being off-balance. Go in for the kill. Do whatever it took to make him submit.

The memory of blood flashed across his vision, and he stumbled.

Parker laughed soot-black smoke as he slunk into the cover of the roaring flames. *Long time no see, kiddo, but you ever think of calling ahead? I'm in the middle of a business deal. I don't need you trying to muscle in.*

I'm not here to steal your business, Fleance snarled. Parker laughed again.

No? What are you here for, then? Don't tell me you've still got a bee in your bonnet over the work we did together. His eyes flashed strangely. *Where is my old buddy Caine, anyway?*

He's not here, Fleance snapped.

That so? Interesting…

Something tugged inside Fleance's head, as though the shadows around his pack-sense were growing thicker. He forced the feeling away, focusing as hard as he could on the dim constellation of his pack. Alarms went off in his head. His pack-sense had been weaker ever since he left the States. He didn't think distance could destroy it entirely, but if it could…

The golden mate bond responded to his fear. It flared bright and shining, a reminder that even if his pack was far away, his mate was close by.

Too close. Dread clamped down on Fleance's heart. She hadn't run away.

Why are you still here? he sent to her, his voice an arrow he hoped Parker couldn't overhear.

She responded at once. *I'm not going to leave you here!*

What made you come all this way, kiddo? Parker's voice twisted around his mind like an icy wind trying to find a way in. *Once was, you couldn't wait to get away from me.*

Then I'll leave, Fleance barked. With Sheena still here—he couldn't risk her.

I don't think so. Parker's eyes burned dark from the flames. *I didn't put on this show for nothing. My original audience might have missed the curtain, but I'm not going to let that gatecrasher out there get away.*

He disappeared. Fleance blinked, his senses on edge. Parker must have phased straight through the wall. He ran after him and burst out from the flames only a few yards behind Parker.

There was no time to plan an attack now. No time to know if his instincts were right. Sheena was standing on the landscaped slope up behind the houses, upwind from the fire. Her pants were ripped at the knee, blood spotting around the tears, and her nostrils flared as she saw the two hellhounds step out of the flames.

Parker took a step towards her and Fleance surged forward, teeth bared. *Don't touch her!*

Fleance leaped. He was smaller than Parker, but this time his aim was true. When he hit the other hellhound, Parker went down like a tree falling. Fleance rolled with him, snapping, clawing, no room in his head for anything other than instant action and reaction.

Parker's claws raked against his belly. Fleance yelped, twisting into a defensive posture. Wrong reaction. Parker moved like smoke. Pain shot through Fleance's face, tearing, hot.

Fleance!

Sheena's shriek cut through the pain. He ripped his head out of Parker's jaws in time to see her swing a plank of wood towards the other shifter.

The plank hit Parker in the neck. He snarled, turning on Sheena, and lunged. Sheena dropped—No, Fleance realized, she *shifted*, becoming small enough to slip beneath Parker's legs. Fleance glimpsed white wool, a black face and flailing ears as she ran. Then Parker snarled with frustration and Fleance took advantage of his lapse in attention to close his jaws around Parker's neck.

He could feel Parker's pulse beneath his teeth. The promise of blood. *Bite down*, his hellhound snarled, *finish this!*

Shock tore through him, as though he was watching himself from above. Finish him?

He was a monster, he knew that. Parker had made him a monster. But...

What are you waiting for? Parker snarled.

I'm here to finish what Caine started. He was playing for time. Ice sweat broke out on his back. *He made you leave. It wasn't enough. You're too dangerous—*

Especially now. Parker looked as though he was rotting from the inside. His outsides finally matched the corruption within. He was a monster.

But Fleance didn't have to kill him. There was another way this could end.

—I have to stop you, he finished.

Parker glared at him, his eyes rolling in his head. Then, to Fleance's mixed horror and confusion, he started to laugh.

Stop me? You? I already told you. You're not man enough.

You have to submit! Fleance growled.

He tightened his jaw, just a fraction. Still not enough to draw blood.

One bite. That was how it worked, wasn't it? One bite had transformed him into a hellhound and made him Parker's slave. When Caine had defeated Parker and taken control of the pack, he'd... he'd...

Fleance's nerves jangled as he realized Caine had never mentioned *biting* Parker.

The other hellhound's throat wobbled beneath his teeth as he laughed.

Flea, Flea, Flea. Always biting off more than you can chew. What do you think is going to happen here? He was grinning, now, his lips stretched back over sharp gray teeth. *Go on! Do it! Just like I taught you, huh? What do you think's going to happen? You'll be the big, bad alpha and have my voice in your head forever?*

Fleance, what's he talking about? Compared to Parker's voice, Sheena's was a ray of sunshine. But she sounded worried. *His voice in your head?*

Go on. Explain it to the poor girl. What you think is going to happen. When Fleance didn't immediately respond, Parker jerked up, almost impaling himself on Fleance's teeth. *It won't work! You'll never control me. Caine was an alpha. Why do you think I didn't bring him to heel after I turned him like I did the rest of you? The risk outweighed the reward. But you… you're just a lackey.* His eyes narrowed. *The most you can hope for is to kill me. But you're too weak to do that, aren't you? Too weak to do what has to be done. Just as you always were.*

Fleance's head was ringing. He released his bite as bitterness flooded his mouth. Angus slunk to his feet, a mocking snarl on his mouth.

No surprises there. Same old Flea, huh? Pathetic.

Fleance felt sick. He hesitated, and that was all Parker needed to act. He twisted and snapped at Sheena before either of them could react.

The smell of blood hit Fleance like a blow. He surged forward, man and hellhound united to protect his mate. A shout echoed in his mind, but all he could focus on was getting between Parker and Sheena. Hellfire dripped from his jaws. He stalked forward, driving the other hellhound back towards the burning buildings.

Parker was limping, but the look on his face was pure malevolence. *You shouldn't have come here,* he snarled.

Fleance growled back at him. He couldn't risk looking back but all of his senses were straining towards his mate behind him. *Sheena,* he sent, taking care to make sure Parker couldn't hear him, *are you hurt?*

I'm— A bitten-off curse that fell like a knife's blade on his ears. *All good. Just gotta shift.*

Her voice was hard and slippery, and he fought against the sudden feeling that she was getting away from him. Parker's voice echoed in his head.

But you turning up does have its benefits. His hound's face split in a sulfurous grin. *With my business partners sadly missing their appointment, I was in for a lonely afternoon.*

"Business—where are my aunts, you arsehole! Why is their house the only one not on fire? What have you done with them?" Sheena yelled. She must have shifted back into human form already. Her voice was hoarse.

Done with them? Nothing. They should be here… Parker swept his muzzle in an arc, a caricature of the concerned host. *People in this country are too laid back, if you ask me.*

"If you've hurt them—"

What will you do? Bleat me to death? Parker laughed again.

Fleance concentrated. *Sheena, I can't smell anyone here but us. There's a strong scent of two people around the one house that hasn't burned down, but it's stale. They must have gotten out before all this started.*

Her relief shuddered down the mate bond.

Parker yawned, his jaw cracking. *They're both shifters, of course, which limited my options, but I didn't think I'd scared them so badly that they'd miss the big day. We're meant to be cracking open the champagne! Doesn't it seem like the perfect time to celebrate doing business together?*

Standing half-in the flames of a burning house, Parker looked as though he'd stepped straight out of hell. Fleance stared at him.

What's wrong with you? What you did back home was bad enough, but this…

This is what it looks like when I don't have anyone holding me back. Parker's eyes gleamed. *Oh, that's right, boyo. Without you whining and crying every time I tried to get ahead, I've been able to move into the big leagues. I'm going to see just how far my luck can take me. And my powers, of course.* His voice was like a nest of worms squirming against Fleance's mind. *But it's a lot of work for one man, so I'm thinking of putting together a team.*

You'll never convince me to come back, Fleance snarled. *That bullshit about me holding you back—that's not true. You never showed any mercy.*

Well, listen to Mr. Too-big-for-his-britches over here! Who said I was talking about you, boyo?

His eyes slid past Fleance to Sheena, and then he vanished in a whirl of stinking smoke. Fleance jerked forwards, but there was nothing to chase—no scent, no sign. It was as though Parker had never been there.

Then a voice whispered in his ear: *Good talking to you, kiddo. We'll have to do this again some time. All three of us.*

And he was gone.

"Is he—" Sheena began, and gasped. Fleance spun to face her, but she was looking over his head. "The fire's stopped."

Fleance turned slowly. The air still smelled of smoke and burned wood, stone, and plastic, but the fire that had been devouring the houses was… gone.

"How is that possible?" she asked.

"I don't know." And the fact that he didn't know worried him. Parker had already shown him once today that there was more to being a hellhound shifter than he knew. Hellhounds had burning eyes and breathed smoke, but control over fire? That was new, and it scared him.

Sheena swore under her breath and took a wobbly step towards him. Her knee buckled beneath her and Fleance shifted and caught her in his arms before she fell.

For a moment, all he could see was golden light.

Sheena was all warmth and softness. She'd shifted without her clothing and without meaning to, Fleance's hand slid over the generous curve of her hips, the other spreading across her upper back between her shoulder blades. Her head was perfectly tucked under his chin and her body molded against hers like they were made to fit each other.

Fleance's breath was ragged. He'd come so close to losing her that for a moment he couldn't force himself to let her go. He breathed in and her scent filled him: sweet and delicate, like nectar-filled flowers and fresh green grass.

She made a soft, longing noise against his neck and Fleance's world turned upside down. Because he wasn't only touching her, she was touching *him*, her arms wrapped around him and her lips hot against the sliver of skin at the collar of his shirt.

The mate bond hummed with wordless need. Sheena tipped her head back and pushed herself onto her tiptoes, losing her balance just enough that she had to press against him to stay upright. Her eyelids fluttered against his cheek; her lips were so close to his he couldn't think of anything else—

"*Ow*," Sheena burst out, wincing. She dropped heavily back only her heels as her whole body hunched over with pain. "Fucking—*ow*. Please tell me that prick didn't literally bite my whole leg off, because that's what it feels like."

Fleance's voice clawed up through his throat. "He bit you?" He shrugged off his jacket and wrapped it around her shoulders. She leaned into his touch, shivering.

"Yeah, when he tossed me around like a freaking chew toy—" She gasped and swore again. "Seriously, you'd tell me if I was hopping around on one leg, right? I don't want to look."

He didn't want to look, either. His body felt hollowed out with fear. Inside him, his hellhound froze in place, eyes wide and staring. If Parker had bitten Sheena—if he turned her—

His fear crackled along the mate bond. No! He couldn't let her know how scared he was. His hellhound burst into action, snaring the emotion before it reached his mate's heart.

Sheena trembled. He helped her sit down. His jacket skimmed the tops of her thighs. It wasn't enough to keep her warm, and it did nothing to hide the wound just above her knee.

He forced himself to look.

His breath stopped. He didn't swear, or cry out, but only because of the many years he'd spent controlling his reactions in front of Parker. He breathed out, gently. Normally.

"It's not that bad," he lied, and couldn't stop his voice from choking up.

"Bullshit." Sheena leaned over, balancing one elbow on his shoulder. She hissed in a breath. "That looks…"

There were three deep gashes in her leg, trailing blood. Tooth marks. They had to be. The scars on Fleance's neck tingled and the edges of his vision went dark.

"…not as bad as I expected." Sheena's voice seemed to come from a long way away. Fleance's vision narrowed as fear rose bitter at the back of his throat. He held it back, determined not to let Sheena feel it before he'd figured out what he was going to say to her.

The future he'd seen so shining and clear in front of him fell away. What replaced it was just as clear, and more horrifying than anything he'd imagined. If Parker turned Sheena…

Sheena was still talking. His hellhound whined, urging him to listen. "My leg's still attached, right? And it's stopped bleeding. Could be better, sure, but could be—" She winced. "—a whole lot worse. Teach me to go running into a fight with some arsehole ten times my size."

She looked up and her eyes widened. Too late, he tried to control his expression the same way he'd controlled his internal emotions. Her lips parted in a question, and he could almost taste her words, as cold and bitter as the dread coiling at the back of his throat: *Why did you let me do it? Why didn't you protect me?*

His heart ached.

But instead of accusing him, she closed her mouth in a tight line and hunched her shoulders. "I'm sorry," she muttered. "Shit, we haven't even known each other for ten minutes and I'm already a fucking dead weight. I… This can't be what you were hoping for in a mate."

Her expression, which until then had shimmered and glowed with every emotion Fleance had felt reflected in the mate bond, closed over. She looked suddenly much smaller than he remembered, wrapped in his jacket, her bare feet turning white on the frozen ground.

Something snapped inside him. Or, more accurately, snapped into place.

She was his mate. And he was *hers*. Parker had hurt her, and he needed to protect her, not malinger over his own fears.

"I never thought I'd have a mate," he said roughly. "I didn't let myself hope for anything. Let alone someone like you."

Her face twisted. "Someone totally hopeless?"

"Someone who would stand up to a man like Angus Parker." He tipped her head back. "You're strong, and beautiful. I'm the one who has failed you."

Her eyebrows drew together. "What are you talking about? You haven't—"

"I let you get hurt." He ghosted his fingertips along her jaw, guilt twisting inside him as his need to touch her warred with the ugly truth he had to reveal. His hard calluses rasped against her soft skin, another reminder that although fate might have decided they were meant for one another, he was so far beneath her he'd spend his whole life catching up.

"It's just a bite. I've had worse."

"Not worse than this." He wrapped his jacket more closely around her shoulders, then gritted his teeth. Delaying tactics. "A hellhound's bite won't just hurt you. It turns you into a hellhound shifter. Like an infection in your soul." He reached for the ugly marks on her leg, holding his hand a scarce inch above her broken skin.

She didn't shrink away. He didn't realize, until she leaned closer to him, that he'd expected her to.

"But I'm already a shifter." She made a sudden, jerky movement. "I'm already a shifter! He can't—he can't take my sheep away. Can he?"

Fleance looked into her eyes. The mate bond fluttered as her emotions caught it. He felt as though his brain was half-frozen, each thought sodden and heavy.

Parker had never targeted shifters before. That had been part of the threat: to keep his pack in line, as much as anything. If they didn't do a good enough job carrying out his instructions to terrify his latest target, Parker would turn them, and finish the job that way. But only humans. Never shifters.

What had Parker said before, when he was talking about Sheena's aunts? *They're both shifters, of course, which limited my options.*

Relief washed through him, a cool, tidal wave that left him feeling light-headed.

"He can't." He pulled his hand away from Sheena's leg and held her close. Her heartbeat thundered against his chest. "It's okay. You're safe. He won't turn you into a monster like we are."

"You're not a monster." Sheena's expression darkened.

Fleance laughed. The noise surprised him. "You don't need to say that. You've seen Parker. You've seen what hellhounds can do. The fire, the terror…" He smoothed her hair, willing her to understand. "You don't need to pretend. I saw the way you looked at me when you thought I was the one who burned this place down."

"Only for a second!" The mate bond twisted, echoing the guilt that flashed through her eyes. Fleance took her hands and hoped she could feel the reassurance he was trying to send back to her.

"It's okay. I get it. You thought I was a monster." She shook her head, but he went on, a wry smile pulling at his lips: "I am. I know that. I've had long enough to come around to that fact. But I'm your monster, now. I'll keep you safe."

A monster who'd been so weak, he hadn't even been able to keep his mate from harm. That changed, now.

The next time Parker tried to hurt Sheena or her family, Fleance wouldn't fail.

4

SHEENA

I'm your monster.

Sheena wasn't sure how she felt about the shiver that went through her at those words. It was a good shiver—in some very localized areas of her anatomy, a close to fucking unbelievably good one—but it was also…

Disappointed?

No, she told herself. Why would she be disappointed that her mate was a mythic shifter of a type she'd never heard of before, who'd just sworn to protect her from anything that might cause her harm? He was big, strong, and powerful in a way that seemed to surround him like an aura. He would protect her. And as recent events had just shown, she bloody needed protecting.

And—fuck it, she was angry, too. Yes, she'd been wary of Fleance when she'd seen his burning eyes. Just for a second. But he was nothing like that other hellhound shifter. His *hellhound* was nothing like that other monstrous, rotting creature. How could he think that—

She took a deep breath that turned into a hiss of discomfort, and Fleance was all concern.

Of course he is, she thought. *Because I'm his mate and as I've just proved beyond all doubt, I'm just as useless as everyone always told me.*

Fleance shifted back into his hellhound form and carried her through the bush to where he'd parked his car. The rental car was shiny and new and currently parked halfway across a paddock. Sheena grimaced automatically. *Tourists...*

She'd have to have a word with him about that. Along with all the other words, among them, *What the hell just happened?*

He let her down and shifted back into human form the moment her feet hit the ground, and whatever else she'd been about to ask, one new question leaped up in front:

"Hold up," she burst out. Geez, bad enough that she was weak and injured. Had her brain totally carked it, too? How hadn't she noticed this before? "You've got clothes on?"

Fleance looked down at himself. He was wearing the same outfit he'd had on earlier: a long-sleeved, gray woolen top that fit him like a glove, and dark jeans. And shoes. Shoes! And... she was wearing his leather jacket.

She stared back towards the village, half-expecting to see her brain left behind on the path.

He'd shifted straight back into human form... *with his clothes.* That was somehow freakier than any of the other shit that had happened today.

"You have got to tell me how you do that," she breathed, her thoughts jumping back to the outfit that had disintegrated around her as she shifted into her sheep form. She tucked her borrowed jacket more closely around herself. It came midway down her thighs, so it wasn't like she was completely naked, and anyway her sheepiness meant she rarely felt the cold—as though her brain was convinced she was permanently wearing her own wool coat—but... "Being able to shift *with* my clothes would have made so much of my life so much less embarrassing."

"I'll teach you how," Fleance said. His eyes flicked to the collar of her jacket and then—ooh—down to where its hem was skimming her legs. Her skin heated up, and not because of any wool-coat-delusion.

That kiss had been incredible. And they were mates. There was more than just kissing involved in that. If Fleance was anything near as good with other parts of his body as he was with his lips...

He cleared his throat. "I'll grab you a pair of pants, too."

"Oh. Sure. Thanks." Sheena blinked. *Not the time,* she told herself firmly, trying not to feel as though she'd just been brushed off. Except how could he brush her off when she hadn't come onto him?

She'd told him she knew he wasn't what he'd expected. How could she be? How could someone as incredible as him have thought he'd end up with an undersized sheep shifter?

She looked down at her leg to distract herself from the rush of exhaustion that thought sent through her. Fleance had opened the passenger side door and she sat down while he hunted through the boot.

"Clothes and a first-aid kit," he declared, coming back around the car with his arms full. She pulled on a sweater that did a better job of covering her everything than his jacket had. He averted his eyes while she got changed and she felt—good? Bad? Confused?—about it.

Not that she wanted to encourage perving, but... they were mates. Shouldn't he *want* to perv at her?

She sure as shit wanted to perv at him. Damn his magical, clothing-shifting abilities. And a quick perv would at least be something normal in the midst of all this...

One minute we're fighting for our lives against some... thing that's burning down everything around us, the next he's lending me a clean pair of socks, she thought. *I'm pretty sure none of my aunts or uncles ever went through anything like this with their mates.*

She pulled on a pair of sweats that felt like she was wearing a sleeping bag on each leg, and carefully rolled up one pant leg to uncover the wound just above her left knee.

The bite hurt like hell, but it was nothing to look at. It wasn't even bleeding anymore. Just sitting there, on her leg (in her leg?), *hurting*.

Fleance made a small, relieved sound as he kneeled down in front of her. She glanced at him, but his face had fallen back into a sort of careful neutrality that she told herself wasn't freaking her out at all.

"Am I going to make it, doc?" she joked.

He almost smiled. He looked up at her, though, his pale eyes warm, and that was good enough. "You're already healing," he said. "The bleeding's stopped. I'll clean this up and bandage it, and you'll be fine." **And you won't turn.** His psychic voice was a warm breeze against her mind.

She smiled at him. "Fine and ready for round two," she said.

He tensed, just for a moment, and Sheena fought to keep a frown off her face. Then something inside him released. Fire kindled behind his eyes.

"Round two," he said, his voice closer to a purr than a growl, "is something I'm going to take care of myself."

Sheena swallowed. *Okay,* she thought, *maybe this whole 'my monster' thing is hotter than I gave it credit for.*

"Now let me see your side." Fleance set down the first-aid kit and gently lifted her borrowed jacket away from her side. It came off sticky—she didn't want to look—but Fleance didn't scream out *My God, your guts are spilling out everywhere,* so it couldn't be that bad.

"This looks like a claw mark," he muttered. "Not deep. I'll clean it."

She focused on the gentle touch of his fingers as he dabbed away the dried blood and sprayed antiseptic onto the scratches. His touch. His gentle care. Not the wound itself, not how much it bloody hurt, not how she'd gotten it—

—*The monstrous dog moved like smoke. She should move. She tried to, but her side hurt, and her sheep tried to go in the other direction, and all four of her legs tried to go in four more directions, and then he was on top of her and it HURT—*

She squeezed her eyes shut. "What is this all about, anyway? Who was that... thing? How did you turn up in the nick of time?"

Fleance looked at her cautiously. "We shouldn't talk about it here."

She'd seen that look too many times before. Anger grabbed at the fear rising inside her and used it to launch itself up.

"I'm fine. Really. Between my sheep and me I've been hurt way worse than this before." *Too sharp*, she thought as the words leaped out. *Too snappish.*

His expression became guarded. Again, not new. *Classic something-he's-not-telling-me*, Sheena thought, and her shoulders went up at the same time her stomach dropped.

He's my mate, she thought. *Aren't we meant to be able to tell each other anything? Isn't that how it's meant to work?*

She knew why he wasn't saying anything. Why he was pushing off answering her questions until later. Because he thought she couldn't cope.

Something thrummed inside her. It took her a moment to recognize it as the mate bond. Bright and shining, new and already slightly battered... and anchoring her to the powerful, red-haired, fire-eyed man kneeling in front of her.

He looked up at her, one hand stretching tentatively towards hers. When she took it, a shiver went through the mate bond, as though she was feeling him step over some sort of marker.

"I told you, I don't think you're weak. I will tell you everything," he said, his voice hushed. "Just..."

His face shadowed over and when he spoke again, it was inside her mind. *Not here and not out loud. It's not safe.*

"But—" Sheena stopped herself. *But that other shifter—Parker—he's gone, isn't he? I can't even smell him anymore.*

And I bet you couldn't smell him clearly before he appeared, either, Fleance replied grimly. *Just because you can't see or sense a hellhound, doesn't mean we're not there."

What? How?

Magic. His jaw set in a grim line as he finished bandaging her side and moved onto her leg. He hesitated slightly, inspecting the bite marks more carefully than he had the scratches. *Hellhounds can pass completely unseen to all senses. He could be here and we wouldn't know it, unless we were part of his pack.*

My sheep couldn't sense him, even when I could. When he was… making me afraid.

Fleance frowned. *I haven't heard of that happening before.*

"Oh, good." Sheena's cheeks heated up. *Just my sheep being its usual unobservant self, then. Forget I said anything.*

So, hellhounds could turn invisible to all the senses—unless you were a part of their pack. That sounded a lot like her flock sense. Except sheep didn't go invisible.

She concentrated. *I can't feel that... that fake fear anymore. And the only shifter I can sense here is you.*

Fleance looked relieved, and his eyes flickered with possessive fire. *Good. Let's get to the nearest city, uh...*

Rotorua?

Right. Find a hotel to hole up in, make sure you're safe, and then I'll... deal with Parker.

She didn't ask what he meant by 'deal with'. Fleance dabbed stinging antiseptic on the scratch on her leg, and carefully wrapped a bandage over it.

That's that, he murmured. *I think... I think you'll be all right.*

Like I said, I've had worse, Sheena began, and pinched her lips together before she could say anything else that might reinforce the impression that she couldn't leave the house without breaking herself in some way.

Arson. Hellhounds. Invisibility powers. Forget traveling the world; this was more adventure than she'd thought possible, here on her own doorstep. What did those old Tourism NZ ads say? *Don't leave home until you've seen the country?* And here she was.

The ad hadn't said anything about getting savaged by a magical shifter before you leave the country, but Sheena's sheep had always had trouble following instructions.

She swung her legs into the footwell as Fleance tidied away the first-aid kit and got in the driver's side. The scratch across her ribs was fine, but her leg ached like a bastard.

The pain was more frustrating than anything else. Another reminder that she was physically more pathetic than literally everyone else she knew. She'd injured herself before. She'd been *bitten* before, and a bite from a fellow sheep shifter had a lot of crunch damage. The monstrous hellhound had barely sliced into her leg at all. And here she was, wincing over a nibble that didn't even need stitches.

It's not even as bad as when I tried to run through that barbed-wire fence, she said to her sheep. *Remember?*

There was no reply. Sheena held her breath.

All her life, even before she first shifted into her sheep form, her sheep had been there. Tucked away in the very heart of her being. Frolicking or dicking around, usually. Now, it was...

Stop hiding! she said suddenly. *I know you're still there, so come out and talk to me!*

She dove deeper into her own heart, hunting for the cotton-wool fluff of her sheep. It had to be there somewhere. It had to be. It couldn't—

She saw a flicker of *something* just out of each and squeezed her eyes tightly shut, concentrating fiercely on it.

A flicker of black-and-white woolliness.

There you are, she thought, relieved. *What are you doing?*

Her sheep twitched its ears at her, but she got the feeling it hadn't actually listened to her. It was as intently focused on her injury as she was.

It probably hurts so much because I'm embarrassed about it, Sheena thought, to herself since her sheep was off in its own world. *I thought I could help, but instead I just got in the way.*

Shh, her sheep muttered. *I'm concentrating.*

You're concentrating? On what?

Shh!

Jeez Louise, all right…

Sheena blinked and focused on the outside world again. *Not* on her leg. She'd whinged about that enough, even if all the whinging had been inside her own head.

Fleance turned on the engine and glanced her way. "Are you all right?"

His voice brushed against her like heat from a home fire. Sheena blinked.

"Oh, fine. Box of birds."

"A box of…" Fleance's face creased with confusion.

"I mean I'm… fine. No worries." Americans understood 'no worries', didn't they?

She shivered as Fleance put the car in reverse and bumped along the uneven farm road. This Parker character had set fire to everything her aunts had worked so hard for and from what she'd gathered, he'd wanted them to be here to watch.

But why? Who would do something like that? An evil son of a bitch, obviously, but that didn't answer the *why. What does Parker get out of destroying their dreams?*

At least Fiona and Rena were safe. They must be, she decided, given how angry Parker had been about not seeing them. Sheena clung to that thought as Fleance drove back onto the motorway.

My aunts are safe, and I have him. My mate.

Her leg still hurt, but it was fine.

Her sheep was still uncharacteristically quiet.

Sheen squeezed her eyes shut. *It's fine.*

Fleance drove as though the devil was on their heels. Which was closer to true than Sheena was comfortable with. She wanted to know more about who Parker was and why he had attacked her aunts, but Fleance didn't say anything until they were in the city.

She didn't remember much of Rotorua itself from the last time she'd traveled there: only a handful of impressions, like photos in an album. The smell. The way steam rose up from the earth and the lake. The Tudor-style Rotorua Museum, like something imported straight from England. And, outside of the city itself, the thermal wonderland of Whakarewarewa, with its geysers, brightly colored silica pools, and bubbling mud.

And the pit she'd fallen into. That wasn't so much *like* a photo memory, as it was a memory backed up on the reg by the *actual* photo of it her mum had kept.

Some things had changed. The museum was closed—surrounded by temporary fencing to keep people away from the façade, an earthquake-proofing safeguard she'd seen in almost every town she'd been through on her way to Auckland. So much of the country's infrastructure had been built without regard for the fact they were bang on a massive fault line.

The hotels were all running full steam, though. Literally. Some had steam hissing from water features in the forecourt, or from the private spas that dug into hot-water bores on the property.

After cruising the streets cursing at *No Vacancy* signs, Fleance pulled up outside a lakefront hotel. His eyebrows pulled together. "Will this work?" he asked.

"Will it *work*?" Apart from staying with relatives, Sheena had been planning on bunking at hostels, here and overseas. *Hotels* hadn't featured in her plans.

Hotels with lakefront views and an on-site spa? Not even on the horizon.

She slapped her pockets, remembering too late that they weren't *her* pockets. "Shit. My wallet—"

"Don't worry about it." Fleance's smile was barely there, but his eyes were warm. "Letting my credit card take a beating is the least I can do. I'm more worried about them letting us in."

Sheena stared at him. "What? Why?"

A few minutes later, they were standing in a warm hotel room. Sheena wriggled her toes happily in the thick carpet. Fleance was still shaking his head.

"I still can't believe they let us past the front door," he muttered as he shut the door behind them. "The way you're dressed—not that you're not—you're—I mean, you look like—not that I think you *are*…"

The intensity that had blazed from him after the fight had faded, leaving him looking as weary and off-footed as Sheena felt. Something inside her softened. Maybe she should have felt worried, that something as simple as New Zealand's lack of concern for proper dress had thrown him, but instead it made her feel more confident. Finally, something where *she* was the expert.

He trailed off, his expression stricken. Sheena held his eyes until she couldn't take it anymore.

"I look like I'm what? Dressed in clothing ten sizes too big for me, with no shoes?" she said, laughter bubbling up. "They must be used to it. Everyone who visits here comes for either the hot pools or outdoor adventure. I bet I'm far from the first person to come in looking like they walked backwards through a hedge."

"That's not what I was talking about." Fleance moved closer to her. Somehow, here inside this room instead of out in the wilderness, the contrast between their heights seemed much greater. His voice roughened. "I meant it was obvious you were wearing my clothes."

Sheena felt split between two selves. On the one hand they were *meant* to be together. The roughness in his voice, the way his pupils blew out dark and wanting when he looked at her—it was all normal stuff. Right? They were mates. Of course he found her sexy. Hopefully as devastatingly sexy as she found him. And there was no question of whether this path they were going down was the right one. However brash or tentative they were, it was all going to work out.

On the other hand... It was all so new. Her veins hummed with excitement just being near him, and who the hell cared if they knew how it would end up? They were only at the beginning. There was so much more ahead of them, whether they went for it brashly or tentatively or by going straight for a pash in the middle of a street full of burning houses.

She tipped her head back—and back further—to look up at him. "That can't be too rare either," she pointed out. "Once you get past the smell, Rotorua's a pretty romantic place. It's easy to see how people might end up losing their clothes even if they weren't shifters."

Fleance's ears were going pink. "I…"

Should I do this? Sheena didn't wait for her sheep to reply. Like it would have anything useful to say, anyway. *Fuck it.*

"I could lose my clothes now, for example," she breathed, leaning closer to him.

He closed the space between them in an instant. Desire darkened his eyes, overwhelming his raw embarrassment. Sheena tipped her head back, anticipation thrumming beneath her skin. Inevitable or not, every look, every touch, was brand new and exciting.

Fleance lowered his face towards hers. His arms went around her, strong and warm. Sheena held back; much as she wanted to climb him like a tree, she wanted this, too, him *wanting* her, coming to *her*.

He hesitated, his lips so close to hers she could feel his breath as he said:

"We shouldn't."

"What?" Sheena jerked back, confused and clinging to that confusion, because the other major emotion welling up inside her was dread. *Did I do something wrong?*

"Not because I don't want to," Fleance said quickly. He smiled crookedly, and the stumbling passion that Sheena felt through the mate bond made her dread melt away. "Don't ever think that. But I promised you that I would explain about Parker, and hellhounds, and everything. And…"

His voice halted. She didn't need the mate bond to see how hard it was for him to continue, but she didn't know how to convince him to go on, either. She'd spent so much of her life keeping people at a distance. Now that she'd found someone she wanted to come close to, she felt as though she was picking her way through a dark room. She couldn't see her way forward and she couldn't see all the obstacles in her way, and she didn't even know what they were—just that they were there.

But that was what the mate bond was for, wasn't it? To show them that whatever the obstacles, Happily Ever After was on its way. Fleance had used it to show her that he wasn't rejecting *her*, just the moment—could she do the same thing?

She picked up his hand from around her waist and twisted her fingers around his. Her chest felt full to bursting. All she had to do was let it out. Right?

How do I know if it's working? It had been easy to push through all her own defenses in the heat of the moment. Finding a connection and grabbing onto it when they were both terrified for their lives—no problem. But now?

"Whatever it is, you can tell me," she said.

Fleance looked down at their joined hands. He closed his eyes and pressed Sheena's knuckles to his forehead, then kissed them.

The ground disappeared from beneath Sheena's feet. She'd seen Fleance's strength and passion already, his halting attempts to slow down, but this tender gentleness almost undid her.

Almost? She let it undo her completely.

She reached out with her heart—and it was easy again, the road ahead as clear and brightly lit as the golden cord that bound them together—and found...

She shuddered.

"I'm sorry," Fleance said, and Sheena's eyes widened as she realized what she'd just felt. It was like he'd closed a door in her face. Was that what it felt like to other people when she put her defenses up? "I told you, I have to explain everything. And

I don't want you—us—to do anything you'll regret once you know the truth."

5

FLEANCE

He hated to push her out, but it was for the best. In the rush of first seeing her and the fight with Parker, he hadn't thought of what it would mean for Sheena to be his mate.

Being with him had already left her injured. He could promise until the sun went down that he would protect her, but the truth was he'd never been able to keep anyone safe. She deserved to know that before they decided what to do next. And until then, he couldn't risk letting her in. With his experience keeping his thoughts hidden from Parker, it was disturbingly easy to avoid her attempts to reach him via the mate bond.

A real mate wouldn't hide from his fated mate like this, he thought bitterly, but kept the thoughts close. Locked away, where no one but him and his hellhound could hear them.

Still, his gut twisted when he saw her react to him closing himself off. An apology was already on his lips when she squared her shoulders and looked him straight in the eye.

"All right," she said, her voice barely wavering. "Everyone's always telling me not to jump into things blind. You pulling back on my reins is just more proof you're my perfect match, eh?"

"I…"

"If we're going to take things slow…" She stepped back and smoothed her hands over her sweater. *His* sweater. Fleance's chest clenched. If this conversation went the way he expected, the shirt and pants Sheena had borrowed from him were the closest anything of his were going to get to being that close to her. "Let's take it *real* slow. I don't know about you, but I could do with something to eat. Healing really takes it out of me. And a shower, cos, you know, rolling around in the dirt tends to…"

She shook her head and winced. "Geez, listen to me rabbiting on. Shower. Food. Sound good?"

Fleance didn't let himself check the mate bond to find out what she was thinking behind her bright-eyed smile. Relying only on her body language made him feel more unmoored than he expected. As unexpected as the sinking feeling in his stomach that the unmoored-ness gave him. He was so used to hating the choking chains that anchored him to another person, that he didn't know what to do with this new feeling.

Get used to it, he told himself firmly as Sheena ordered room service. He held on until she disappeared into the bathroom and then dropped his head into his hands with a groan as he sat down on the bed. *She won't want anything to do with you when she knows the truth.*

For a few minutes, he convinced himself he could handle it. Then Sheena appeared at the bathroom door again, her damp curls dripping onto the shoulders of a plush white bathrobe that cocooned her from neck to ankles. She should have looked ridiculous, wrapped in a robe far too big for her. Instead, she was radiant.

And Fleance was lost.

"Shower's free!" Sheena said brightly. Fleance jumped up. He still couldn't let himself check the mate bond, but the clean, sweet smell of her as she stepped aside to let him into the bathroom was unavoidable. He wanted to—

No. He *had* to control himself. He'd spent too long a slave to his hellhound's vulnerabilities. He wouldn't let her become one, too.

He showered quickly, his nose twitching at the hint of sulfur as he opened the window to help clear the steam. Normal sulfur, he reminded himself. Not the stench that accompanied hellhounds.

When he finally pulled on fresh clothes and went back out to join Sheena, he felt like the shower had added to the weight on his shoulders, not released it. And the sight of Sheena setting out covered plates on the tiny dining table, still wearing the robe, did nothing to help.

He cleared his throat, intending to ask her if she wanted a few more minutes to get dressed, but something about the obstinate tilt of her chin told her that would be a lost cause. His pulse quickened, despite himself. A meal with his mate wrapped only in a robe, sitting overlooking a serene lake, snow-covered hills in the distance... It was picture-perfect. The sort of thing that belonged in a Christmas rom-com, not in his life.

"I brought the table in from the balcony," Sheena said, distributing cutlery. "The wine list said this red was chosen with Rotorua's *unique aroma* in mind, but I figured it would be even better without. Besides, I've had my quota of freezing my arse off today already."

She flashed him a smile that was too quick for him to tell if it was genuine or not and sat down.

Feeling like he was moving through mud, Fleance followed suit. The table was so small their knees almost touched beneath it. Fleance felt his senses start to shut down out of self-defense—all of this, her, her scent, the fact that she was only wearing a robe, was all too much—except at that moment Sheena whipped the covers off the plates and the smell of their meal overwhelmed everything else.

His stomach growled. Sheena groaned out loud.

"I always forget how hungry shifting makes me," she said, reaching for her knife and fork. "And I'm only a sheep—I hope I ordered enough."

Fleance blinked. She'd ordered seared steaks and a seafood platter, and half a dozen sides including a heaped pile of steaming ravioli in butter sauce and a crispy noodle salad. Two slices of chocolate cake fought for space at the very edge of the table.

"I should have gone for the cheese platter, too," she muttered, worried. "Oh, shit. I forgot you're the one paying for this."

"Don't worry about—"

"I'll pay you back, okay? As soon as I get my stuff back."

"Really, don't worry about it." He caught her gaze and tried to smile. "What's mine is yours."

She didn't look reassured. "Right. Well... it's kai time. Food time. Let's focus on that because whatever you've got to say, I feel like I'm going to need to hear it on a full stomach. Here, try these prawns..."

They both filled their plates. Fleance tried to focus on the food, which was excellent, but he couldn't keep his attention away from her.

She was so beautiful. No, that wasn't the right word, either. She was so... much. He already knew what she looked like, but that was a staccato series of impressions, hyper-focused by adrenaline and outlined in fire. This was the first chance he'd had to slow down and look at her properly.

Her freckled skin was a few shades darker than his—not hard, given he turned invisible in snow even without his hellhound powers—and her hair was an incredible mass of thick curls that just brushed her shoulders. Her eyes were a hazel brown flecked with gold that reminded him of that first intoxicating taste he'd gotten of her scent—like rolling hills of golden grass speckled with shadows.

But she was more than that. What she looked like, her scent—he'd known that within a second of meeting her. And then he'd discovered that she was the sort of woman who refused to run and leave him, who'd jump into a fight no matter how outmatched she was and try to help a man she'd only just met. A man whose job should be protecting her, not the other way around.

She was someone who looked at Parker like he was a monster, and at Fleance like he wasn't.

Somehow, in the years he'd been a shifter, he'd gotten the idea that the mate bond was the final step in finding your mate. Perhaps it was because theirs had sprung into existence so quickly—and the feeling of that happening, of Sheena's heart seizing his with gleeful ferocity, still took his breath away—but all the mate bond told him now was how much he still had to learn about this woman whose soul was bound to his.

She deserved better.

Cold sweat broke out on the back of Fleance's neck. Sheena gasped, and he realized he'd let too much slip. He was used to keeping his emotions hidden beneath the surface of his mind, but he hadn't yet mastered keeping them from reaching Sheena through the mate bond.

"Sorry," he muttered. "I'm still getting used to… everything."

"It's a lot," she agreed. She licked a smear of sauce from the corner of her lips and helped herself to another serving of ravioli. "I mean… on top of everything else I've never even heard of shifters that can turn into animals that don't exist. I'm still getting my head around it."

"You haven't met any mythic shifters before?" When she shook her head, Fleance whistled. "Hellhounds aren't the half of it. Where I live now, Pine Valley—"

"Pine Valley? Is that exactly what it sounds like?" When Fleance nodded, Sheena snorted. "Good to know other countries are as good at naming stuff as we are."

"It's become something of a hub for mythic shifters. Makes sense, I guess, given one of the oldest families there is a dragon clan."

Sheena almost choked on her drink. "Dragons?"

"The Heartwell clan lives in the mountains above the town. A brother and sister, and their families." He hurried to clarify as Sheena's eyes got wider. "*Small* families. They only have one child each, and Jasper's mate isn't a shifter, so it's only five dragons."

"*Only* five dragons." Sheena sounded like she was testing out the words. "Only *five* dragons. Only five *dragons*. What next? Wizards?"

"Not that I wouldn't pay good money to see a guy shift into a guy with a longer beard and a pointy hat, but—" He put his head on one side. "You did know dragon shifters exist?"

"No!"

"But..." Fleance waved out the window, where the lake was steaming gently. "This is *Lord of the Rings* country. You've got volcanoes, sulfur pools—how are you not crawling with mythical shifters?"

"It's seriously mostly sheep." Her eyes were still like saucers. "But... dragons?"

Fleance couldn't help but laugh. "Our sheriff is a pegasus shifter."

"Okay, now you've got to be joking."

"He used to work with a guy who could turn into a griffin."

"A—no." Sheena folded her arms. "Seriously? I've never even heard of mythical shifters. Sure, there

are stories about taniwha, but those are… taniwha."
His confusion must have shown on his face, and if
he needed any proof that she was the other half of
his soul, that was it. He would never have let his
emotions show so easily in his old life. Now, he
hadn't even noticed how easily his mask had slid off.

Sheena unfolded her arms to gesture. "Taniwha
are… They're mythical guardians. Of waterways,
usually. *Actual* myths, not real the way shifters are
real, though don't tell my cousin Aroha I said that."
Mid-gesture, her hands seemed to arrive near her
head by accident, and she ran them through her
curls. "But… actual, real mythical shifters. Wow.
The closest I've ever gotten to something like that
is wondering if people could be shifters of extinct
animals, or only ones that are alive now." She looked
at him, slightly worried.

"I've never met a dinosaur shifter," he reassured
her.

"Oh, just dragons and pegasuses and hellhounds.
No worries." She picked up her fork and stabbed
another ravioli. "And… Are you the only hellhound
who lives there?"

"No. It's me and the rest of my pack. My alpha,
Caine Guinness, and his mate Meaghan have lived
there for a while. The rest of us are newcomers." He
didn't mention that he'd slunk away without telling

his alpha where he was going. But Caine was smart. He must have guessed.

So long as he doesn't come over himself or send any of the others. Parker is my responsibility.

"'The rest of your pack.' You keep talking about your pack, and *alphas*. What's that about? And... you live on the other side of the world, and you somehow managed to turn up at Silver Springs the moment I needed you. How is that possible?"

Left unsaid: *If he'd been a day late...* He pushed the thought away and made his voice light.

"A hunch."

"A *hunch?*"

Fleance met Sheena's eyes and something shivered inside him. A door he hadn't even known he'd kept locked trembled against its hinges.

"It was more than a hunch. I've known Angus Parker for a long time."

"You've been chasing him?"

"I know his tactics." *That's one way of putting it. So close to the truth that it's an even worse lie.* Fleance cleared his throat. "Parker has made a career out of using his powers to force people into corners so he could trick them into bad contracts. He started off by terrorizing individuals or small businesses into folding. But after a while, that wasn't enough. A few years ago, he targeted Pine Valley. It's a small tourist town, way off the beaten track. The perfect test case to see if he could take on a whole community." Fleance stared at his wine glass, unable to meet Sheena's eyes. "And it would have worked if there wasn't another alpha hellhound already there. Caine Guinness caught on to what Parker was doing, fought him, and forced him to leave Pine Valley in peace." He sighed. "Without another alpha to fight him, I don't think even the dragons could have taken Parker out."

"And you fought him then, with this Caine guy?"

Fleance hesitated. *Parker bit her, but she's already a shifter. She won't turn.* The thought wound itself eel-like around his spinal column. *I don't need to tell her everything. That Parker's dangerous, yes, that I'll keep her safe, yes... but I can keep the rest a secret.*

Who I really am.

What I did.

What I came here to do, and failed to do, and what I'll have to do now instead.

I have to lie to her. Because who would want to be tied to what I really am?

His shoulders tightened. *No.* Parker might have made him a monster, but he didn't have to act like one. He wouldn't be with her under false pretenses.

He looked across at her. Now that he'd soaked in what she looked like, finer details sprang to the forefront: the slight tremor in her hands as she sipped her wine; the dark smudges under her eyes and the way her expression sometimes slipped, just briefly, and one hand flew to hover painfully an inch above her leg where Parker had bitten her.

"You're a sheep shifter, right?"

Her eyebrows went up. "Valais blacknose, present and accounted for. My whole family are. I can't turn invisible, or—or make people afraid of things that aren't there, or set fires that magically disappear. My special ability is being so bloody cute no one takes me seriously." She bit her lower lip. "So, please, take me seriously. Tell me what's going on here, or at least—tell me about yourself. Because right now I'm terrified. I left my wallet, my phone, everything back at Silver Springs and I don't know what's happening with my aunts, and…" She took a too-quick glug of wine and wiped a spill from the side of her mouth. "I know I sound like a scared kid right now but I could *really* do with some reassurance."

"You don't sound like a scared kid."

"I feel like one." She made a face. "I've spent the last three months convincing everyone who knows me that I can look after myself, and I didn't even have to leave the country to find out that's not true." She bit her bottom lip. "I'm just glad you're here. Whatever that arsehole back at Silver Springs had in mind… I wouldn't have made it out without you."

She thinks I'm some sort of hero, Fleance thought, guilt twisting in his gut. *She doesn't know that if it wasn't for me, Parker never would have been here in the first place.*

"If it helps, I'm certain your aunts are safe," he said out loud. "I know the way Parker works. He'll terrorize people, but he's never left a body count."

Sheena flinched at the words *body count*, and Fleance cursed himself. Before he could say anything else, she put down her glass with a *clonk* and rubbed one hand across her forehead.

"You know so much about who this guy is. Are you some sort of shifter detective, or something?"

Fleance's throat went dry. He was meant to be telling her the truth, not letting her come up with tempting lies. But that was what he'd done for so many years: let his mind be smooth as a pond as he slid in Parker's wake, not letting his alpha see any trace of his true thoughts.

Not anymore. Not with her.

"I wasn't part of Caine's pack then," he began.

"You keep saying 'pack' like I should know what that means," Sheena interjected.

He frowned. "Sheep shifters are pack animals, aren't they?" he asked.

"Uh, flock animals, sure."

"Then you know that some shifter groups have particular... structures. Hellhounds are extremely pack-oriented. The alpha has control over all the subordinate hellhounds."

Sheena scowled. Somehow, that made Fleance feel like he was on more solid ground. Her frown took over her entire face. It was a whole, all-in expression, everything that tentative smile hadn't been.

"Control?" she asked. Even her *voice* was a frown.

"An alpha leads their pack. It makes sense they couldn't do that without some sort of force. And with hellhounds, that force is magical. We all serve our alpha. And until Pine Valley, Parker was my alpha."

Sheena gasped. "No."

The smile that stretched across his face felt like a sick, sour thing. "When Caine defeated Parker, he took control of his pack, too. Me, Manu and Rhys."

"Manu—isn't that a Māori name?"

Fleance recognized the word—Māori were the indigenous people of New Zealand. Manu's people.

"Where do you think Parker got the idea to use New Zealand as his bolt hole?"

Sheena leaned back in her chair. She'd gone pale beneath her freckles. "So you came here to... to..."

The truth. He groaned and ran his fingers through his hair. "To serve my pack. I thought, wrongly, that I could serve them best by coming here and dealing with Parker, but instead I've just let Parker know that the pack's in a vulnerable position. Enough so that I would risk leaving them to come here and do something about him."

Something. He had to stop dancing around it.

Bite down, his hellhound had told him. *Finish him!*

Sheena didn't look reassured. In fact, every time he mentioned pack dynamics, or alphas, her expression became surlier. "Well, is he right about your pack being vulnerable?"

"Caine's mate, Meaghan, is pregnant. Twins. She's due later this month. If Parker did want to have his revenge on Caine for taking the pack from him, this would be the perfect opportunity. Everyone will be distracted." Cold crept up the back of his neck. "And if it wasn't for me, he'd have no idea."

"But he still doesn't, right? You didn't actually tell him about the babies. Which, congratulations, by the way." She grinned, genuine pleasure sparkling in her eyes.

Fleance wanted more than anything to return her smile. Instead he shook his head. "Parker's a cut-throat businessman. And his business is finding other people's weak points. He doesn't need to know what the vulnerability is, just that they have one. Any weakness is an opportunity." His neck muscles tightened. "Parker might say he had no interest in his old pack, but I know better. And if there's any chance that Parker might take back control of the pack—if he gets any power over Caine and Meaghan's kids, or even over Rhys and Manu again—"

"Or you." Sheena's expression was caught in that uneasy space between extremes again. "That's what this is about, isn't it? Parker used to be your alpha, and everything you've said about him using his hellhound powers to do evil business deals... What did he do to you? I—*ow*."

She winced. Fleance's hellhound jumped to attention. *What's wrong?* he asked quickly, and she raised her hands.

"Nothing! It's—*ow*—just my leg. It's itching really badly." She made a face. "Sorry. I didn't mean to interrupt."

"It was yourself you interrupted."

"You know what I mean." She said it with a weak half-smile that looked out of place on her face. Her eyes were shining. Fleance looked away.

"Stop looking at me like I'm some sort of hero."

"Why? You sound pretty damn heroic to me." Her voice had an edge to it that went straight to Fleance's core. "I can't imagine that Parker having any sort of power over you was a barrel of laughs. But you still came here, to protect the people you care about."

"And failed." He worked his jaw, as though the truth was something he could physically spit out. Inside him, his hellhound whined. It didn't want to tell her the truth.

Where's your outsized sense of justice now? he asked it bitterly.

Sheena was still watching him. Not warily, but intently. He couldn't meet her eyes.

"You saw what happened back there. I... thought I knew what I was doing. I thought I could defeat him. I should have known better."

"...What *were* you trying to do?" Sheena picked up her knife and fork, and Fleance couldn't help thinking that she was just *trying* to act normally. Like everyone did, when faced by hellhounds. Promising herself that if she just kept acting like nothing was wrong, her magical thinking would make the world a less scary place. "When you were fighting... You two were really going at it." She trailed off, awkwardly.

"I thought I could force him to not hurt anyone anymore," Fleance said. "Like Caine forced him to free us and leave Pine Valley. But I'm no alpha. I should have known it wouldn't work." The words felt like gravel in his throat. He ate a forkful of food without tasting it and washed it down with the wine. The menu hadn't been joking about it being selected to compete with Rotorua's pungent air; the wine was so strong he almost choked.

"It's a bit overpowering, huh?" Sheena waited for him to stop coughing. "What do you mean, you could force him to stop hurting people? You mean using that... fear magic?" She shivered. "You'd need to constantly chase him around, herding him away from people."

"Not exactly. I'd thought—" Fleance broke off. What had he thought? He'd been so set on coming here, but what had he really planned to do once he arrived?

I thought that just because I was free, I could take control of him like he did me. Force him to swear he'd never hurt anyone again.

No. That's just what I told myself. His skin prickled as he looked out the window, across the steaming lake. *You know what you came here to do*, a voice in his head sneered. It wasn't his own voice, or his hellhound's. It sounded so much like his uncle, his fists clenched. *You tried to tell yourself a story, but you knew all along what this would come to. Parker knew, too. And he knew you'd never go through with it.*

You're no alpha. You can't command another hellhound. There's only one way to stop Parker.

"You said Parker controlled the hellhounds in his pack, and *you* were in his pack. You're so scared of what he might do to your new alpha's children that you came all the way to the other side of the world to confront him. What—what did he do to you?"

The bond of light between them pulled at Fleance's chest, as though she was trying to psychically draw him closer. If it wasn't for the table between them, Fleance might have crumbled to temptation and let himself be drawn.

Then Sheena winced again and rubbed her leg, and that one reminder of how he'd failed to protect her gave Fleance the strength to hold back.

The scars on his neck itched in sympathy as Sheena clutched her leg. He stopped himself from scratching them; the last thing he wanted was to draw Sheena's attention to them. Instead he sat up straight, hands clenched hidden under the table.

"I wasn't some innocent victim. I was part of Parker's pack for years. The *first* member of his pack. I already told you what Parker's game is. Using his hellhound powers. Turning invisible, walking through walls, making people afraid just by our very presence—in his hands, those powers were weapons." He flexed his own hand, staring at it as though he'd never seen it before. "Except he didn't like to get his hands dirty. We were the ones who scared people. Who hunted them down and terrified them until they'd do anything to get out. And Parker was always there, waiting in the light with the contract and a pen ready for them to sign away everything they valued."

He wasn't looking at his hand anymore. He was looking into the past. Every painful moment of it. "He always made sure that while the worst of it was going down, he was seen somewhere else.

So that even if someone did dare to mention they thought they were being followed by creatures that disappeared into thin air, or their homes and businesses were trashed but there was no sign of a break in, doors and windows still locked tight, people would think they were crazy. And if the authorities did think there was something to it, there wouldn't be any proof Parker was involved. Not when he had been busy at a charity function or filming an interview about his not-for-profit work." Bitterness tightened his throat. "He always got away with it. Whatever he wanted, he took."

"And you couldn't go to the authorities? Even here there are a few shifters in the police. They can't put it in the official books, but they help when shifters are using their shapeshifting abilities to break the law."

"Would they believe the rest of it? Even shifters have trouble accepting what we can do." Fleance knew he sounded defeated. He *felt* defeated. Remembering his past was like pulling on an old coat that was perfectly worn into the shape of his body. He'd managed to shake it off for a few brief years, but now... "We could have shown people what we could do, but Parker had thought of that, too. He made sure we behaved. Forced us to keep our powers secret. And eventually..."

He looked down at his hands. "I want to say that I fought him all the way. But I didn't. I told you I'm not blameless. I had more chance than any of the others to fight back, and I never acted. You need to know that. I'm no hero. That's Caine, my alpha. I'm just…" His shoulders sank. "Here to try to do what's right, for once in my life."

When he forced himself to look at her, she didn't look convinced. He took another mouthful of the paint-stripping wine and squared his shoulders. "I'll explain from the beginning. Maybe then you'll understand."

"Maybe." She looked troubled.

"When I was eighteen, my parents died in a car crash," he began, and Sheena jerked.

"Jeez! I mean—sorry." She stumbled over her words, but the swell of light down the mate bond told Fleance everything she wanted to say. "I'm sorry."

He shook his head. "It was a long time ago—"

"Still."

"Still," he echoed her. "Thank you. But that's not—important. It's just to set the scene, so that you understand what happens next." As though his life was a screenplay, where every page of action made sense. He swallowed. "I'd just moved out of home. The last thing my parents and I did before I left for college was pack up all the shit in my room—my uncle was coming to stay while he was in town for business, and Dad joked that if he did his own laundry they might just keep him, and I could fend for myself over the break.

"I got the call in the middle of my first class. I hadn't even unpacked my bags. There'd been an accident…"

He broke off. "I didn't hear the details. Or I don't remember. I still don't know if anyone actually told me exactly what happened, or how, just… It didn't matter, anyway. I couldn't stop thinking about that last joke my Dad made. Then I was home again, and they were both dead, and the only reason I wasn't left to fend for myself was that Uncle Angus was staying, after all. He managed all the—the legal stuff. I tried to go back to college, but I couldn't cope. Mom and Dad had given up so much so I could get into a good school, and I couldn't even finish my first year."

"No one could blame you for that."

"I could. I couldn't *not* blame myself. What happened to my parents was so random, so unexplainable, I thought at least if I could blame myself for something I *could* have controlled, I'd…" He shook his head. "I don't know what I thought. It felt like it made sense at the time."

He should be angry at his past self, he knew that. But those days were the last he'd had as *himself*. He'd been young and stupid and thoughtless—and human.

Inside him, his hellhound shivered and whined softly.

"And at the same time as all that was happening... My uncle was there. No matter what was falling apart, he was there for me. Maybe I should have been more suspicious of that, but I was just glad to have anybody. I'd only met him a few times before. A couple of Thanksgivings, a summer holiday when I was in elementary school. Mom said he was always too busy with work to be around much, but he was the only family I had left and when he stepped in, I thought it was just because that's what family does." Fleance paused. He'd never talked about any of this and now, it seemed too easy. The words kept coming, slipping out as thought they had a life of their own. "He arranged for my parents' home to be sold, gave me a place to live in a new city, and... offered me a place in the family business. I didn't even ask what the business was. I was sick of being sad and useless and—I wanted to show Uncle Angus that I was worth all the time he'd spent on me."

"That makes sense," Sheena said awkwardly. Her fingers tightened around his hand. "Awful sense, but—you were a kid and you'd just lost your parents. Of course you trusted him, of course you wanted him to stick around."

"I would have done anything for him." Fleance stared down at his plate without seeing it. "I told him so, and he said… he was glad to have me on board. I thought he was offering me a job. I told him I didn't have any experience. I wanted him to be proud of me. I wanted to show him I could be useful. I was going to give college another go, get a degree in business studies, but…"

His uncle had gone along with it, that was the worst thing. He'd let Fleance fill his head with dreams, while he put his own plans in motion. And then the timer had run out.

"…that didn't happen. My uncle took me out on a fishing trip one weekend, to this cabin way out in the woods. He said he had two days off before his next business deal, so I guess that's why he didn't waste any time. The moment we were out of the car, he shifted and attacked me."

Clang!

Sheena dropped her wine glass. Red wine spilled over the table, but she barely noticed.

"He *attacked* you?" Her eyes opened wide. "Wait—we were talking about Parker. Your uncle isn't…"

"Angus Parker. My mom's brother. And my old alpha."

He'd expected her to back away, but instead, she stood up so quickly she bumped the table. The wine bottle only just remained upright as she stumbled around and grabbed the front of Fleance's shirt in both hands.

"You could have *led* with that, you know!" she exclaimed. "You—" She stretched out both hands flat against his chest, fingers wide, as though she was trying to hold his heart in place. "You…" she repeated, and a blush spread across her face. She dropped her hands. "Sorry," she muttered, grabbing her chair and pulling it around the tiny table until it was jammed close against his, "but in my defense, you can't just bloody say something like that! Parker is your *uncle?* And he treated you like that?"

Instead of backing away, she dropped into the chair, eyes fixed on his.

"Yes," Fleance said, not sure whether his brain was falling behind his mouth or it was the other way around. Sheena swore and took his hand.

"Then I can guess that whatever happened next, isn't good. He attacked you? Why?"

"He… wanted me to join the family business. *His* business. I told you he used his pack to do his dirty work. He started with me."

"So he… let me get this straight. He attacked you to control your hellhound, and because he was an alpha and you weren't, you had to do what he said?"

"No, he—" Fleance rubbed the scar on his neck reflexively. Sheena's eyes tracked the motion and when she saw the marks on his neck, she went very still. "I already told you hellhound shifters aren't born. They're made. It's like an infection," he said, and deep inside him, his hellhound shivered with shame. "And Angus Parker turned that infection into a key business practice."

"He… *turned you*? Your own uncle? You *trusted* him, and you'd just lost your parents, and—" Her face twisted, and she grabbed him by the shoulders. "He's a monster. No wonder you came after him to protect your pack. I want to kill him myself!"

He gently eased her hands from his shoulders. Somehow, he didn't quite manage to let them go. "I know I'm making myself sound like the victim. But I was the one who walked straight into Parker's trap. And then I *became* part of the trap. Everything he did? Terrorizing people into leaving their homes, destroying their lives? That was *me*. I hurt people. And then, when Parker turned Rhys and Manu—"

"You must have tried to stop him," Sheena protested.

"I didn't. I *couldn't*. I tried, when he started turning the others to add to his pack, but trying isn't *doing*. There was nothing I could do to save any of us." His muscles were so tense, Fleance felt as though he was encased in a suit of armor. "Everything Parker did, he managed because I was there to help him. I'm as culpable as he is. I couldn't stop him then, I wasn't strong enough, but even after my new alpha broke

Parker's control I didn't do anything to put right the damage he caused. My hellhound…"

He dropped her hands. His hellhound hadn't said a word since he said that being turned into a hellhound was like an infection. He could feel it listening, so intent it was shaking.

"…My hellhound has been having problems since last Christmas," he said. "I thought at first that it was broken, somehow, that after everything else Parker had left me with a part of my soul that wanted to hurt people like he made me do. But *I'm* the broken one. I saw everything that Parker did and when I had the chance to finally put an end to it… I did nothing. I hid behind my new alpha and told myself I'd put the past behind me. Like it wasn't anything to do with me anymore."

"You're being too hard on yourself." Sheena's words struck the shell he'd constructed around himself like rocks. "You just said he forced you to do all those things. And he's your *uncle*. You didn't fail anyone. You weren't hiding, you were recovering." She tucked her hands into the too-long sleeves of her robe and scowled. "I was born too early. Some of my organs weren't even finished growing. Which means I've been sick enough of my life to know that you have to be easy on yourself while you're getting over bad stuff. My bad stuff was mostly my lungs, not my—"

"Not your soul." Fleance didn't mean to interrupt. He didn't mean for the words to come out jagged-edged and bitter, either, but that didn't stop them. "Being easy on myself didn't help, it made it worse. And knowing there was nothing I *could* do doesn't help. It didn't stop my hellhound from attacking people to try and make them stop breaking the rules, because it spent so long unable to stop my uncle, and it doesn't help…"

He stared at Sheena's thigh, as though he could see through the fluffy bath robe to the bandaged bite marks beneath. Even if Parker couldn't turn Sheena, he'd proved to Fleance how weak he still was in comparison to his uncle. "It didn't help you. Parker is still hurting people, and after today, I can't avoid the truth anymore. I know what I need to do."

Sheena frowned. "Parker said you couldn't control him because you're not an alpha. Are you going to ask this guy Caine to come all the way here?"

"No. I'm going to kill Parker myself."

6

SHEENA

"You want to kill him?" Sheena was suddenly very glad they'd decided to eat at the hotel. The words came out far louder than she'd planned and that was not the sort of thing you wanted to say in a restaurant. "That's… a bit dark. And illegal. Er, a lot illegal."

I sound like the scared girlfriend in some B-grade action movie, she thought as the words leaped out of her mouth. Her heart was hammering. She wanted to tell herself that she'd misheard him, that this was all a mistake, but the expression on Fleance's face left no room for her to lie to herself.

"I don't want to do it. But I don't see any other way out." Fleance stared out over the lake. The sun had set and the city lights only just touched the steam rising from the water, giving the impression that there was something out there, wrapping itself around the town. Fleance's expression became guarded. "When Caine took over from Parker, I thought that was it. New alpha, blank slate. But my hellhound won't rest until I've done something about him."

"*Done something* doesn't have to mean murder, though," Sheena said, and Fleance flinched.

"I have to make sure he's not going to come back and hurt anyone. You've already seen what he did to your aunts. And... if I can't stop him, I'm worried I won't be able to stop my hellhound from being a danger to everyone around me."

Sheena's heart sank as Fleance told her what his hellhound had been like the last few months. Jumping at shadows, overreacting to the slightest misdemeanors.

"It stopped as soon as I connected the dots. Parker was the reason my hellhound was acting up. It couldn't reach him, so it was transferring its need to put things right to anyone it could reach." His mouth formed a grim line. "I didn't like who I was under Parker's control and I didn't like who I was when my hellhound wanted to chase down every poor asshole who accidentally knocked someone over or—hell, pulled a dog's tail. Any damn thing. I don't like the idea of—what I have to do here, either, but I know it's what I'm meant to do. Parker made sure of that when he made me what I am. Maybe once I'm done here... I'll find peace." Bitterness threaded through his voice.

Sheena shuffled her chair closer to his, wincing as her leg twinged. He hesitated as she leaned against his side, then put his arm around her, fast, as though he was afraid she'd move away.

He buried his face in her hair and breathed in deep. "And I'll be protecting you, too. That is the right thing to do. Knowing you're safe will bring me peace."

"There *has* to be another way." A knot formed in her stomach. Her fated mate couldn't be a murderer. No matter how trapped Fleance felt, or how guilty he felt about what Parker had put him through—which was a whole other steaming pile of shit Sheena had to hold herself back from slamming her fist into—there had to be an alternative.

That's not just me being sheltered, though, is it? After all, she'd never had to deal with anything like what Fleance had been through. She was a sheep shifter from a huge, overprotective family who'd gotten over the worst life had to throw at her before she could walk.

Until now.

I thought finding your mate was supposed to make things simple, she thought suddenly, and was ashamed of the heat that flooded up behind her eyes. She groped blindly for her sheep. Despite how flighty it was normally, it was always there for her when she was down, and right now she needed its wooly reassurance more than ever before.

But it wasn't there.

"There's something wrong with my sheep," she blurted out.

Fleance's arms stiffened around her. God, this was the last thing he needed—he'd just spilled his heart out and she was making it all about her.

She shouldn't have said anything. Bloody drama queen, overreacting to everything.

What do you mean by 'something wrong'? Fleance's voice was tight, and the mate bond twisted in Sheena's chest.

It's nothing. I shouldn't have— Her thigh muscles spasmed. "Ow!"

She hissed and grabbed her thigh. Every time it had hurt before, she'd managed to stop herself from actually touching it, but this time she dug her fingers in around the edges of the bandage as though she was trying to tear it off. Tear off the bandage and the searing pain and the—the—

The cold, empty silence inside her where her sheep had always been, ever since she could remember.

Dread crept up her spine. She felt it crawl along the mate bond, cold and draining, but she couldn't stop it. "I know I said before that everything was fine, but it's... not. I don't know why my sheep wasn't scared when Parker was trying to herd me to a fiery death, but it did get scared as soon as he bit me, and now it's… it's not talking to me at all. And my sheep is *never* this quiet. So whatever's happening now… I'm scared. Really scared and—and now I'm bloody running my mouth and that's not going to help, is it, and… and part of me is asking me why I'm even telling you all this stuff, because I'd never tell *anyone* back home if I was scared, or weak, but… you're my mate. I'm meant to tell you stuff like this. Aren't I?"

"Yes." Fleance's voice sounded as though his throat was full of stones. "And you're not weak. No one could think that."

"I *feel* weak." She felt as though her body was sucking into itself, becoming brittle and fragile beneath the smothering white dressing gown. She'd deliberately not gotten properly dressed because she thought she knew which way this evening was going to go. What a joke. "And I *hate* it." She swallowed, her mouth a tight, unhappy line. "I hate feeling as weak and useless as everyone thinks I am."

Fleance wrapped his hand gently over her leg, where the bandaged bite was covered by her dressing gown.

Sheena… Fleance tipped her head up so she was looking into his eyes. They were gray-blue, without a trace of hellhound fire. *You're not weak. You're going through something no shifter—no person—should have to endure. A hellhound attacked you. Weren't you just* *talking about being easy on yourself when you're getting over bad stuff?**

She swallowed, her throat suddenly dry. *That was advice for you, not advice for me. I—*

Her leg throbbed, and images filled her mind. A rush of rotting black fur. The fetid, sweet stink, like a weeks-old dead thing rolling over in brimstone-bubbling water. Her sheep trying to run. Claws scraping the ground. Teeth. Teeth that seemed too big for the creature's sunken jaws, flashing close, jaws wide as a tunnel's mouth—

"Fuck this," she muttered, and pulled her dressing gown up so she could get at the bandage. She tore it off. "I've *had* bites before. None of them hurt for this long. Something's wrong."

"No, it can't be—"

They both fell silent.

The wound was clean. It had started scabbing over, which accounted for some of the scrabbling, itchy pain, but something was clearly wrong.

Dark lines ran out from the three sharp cuts in her leg.

"No," Fleance whispered, his voice hoarse.

"It looks infected." Sheena's voice whined in her ears, tight and nasal. "But it can't have gone that bad so quickly, could it? It feels... hot..."

She trailed off. Fleance's face had gone gray. He rubbed the back of one hand over his eyes as though he was trying to change what he was seeing.

"It's exactly what mine looked like," he said. His voice was as ashen as his face he lifted one hand to shiver across a row of scars on his neck and shoulder. Sheena had noticed them before, but now she guessed without him saying anything what they were. Bite marks. "I thought I was dying. Out in the middle of nowhere, attacked by a wild animal. I had no idea about shifter healing. I had no idea about *shifters*. I thought I was bleeding out and I think it being a dangerous wound meant I turned more quickly, because Rhys only got bitten on the hand, and it took weeks for his hellhound to... You don't want to hear this," he said, suddenly changing course. He pressed the heel of his hand hard against his forehead and groaned. His voice cracked into a pained rasp. "I should have gotten us both out of there the moment Parker appeared. If I'd acted faster, I could have kept you safe. I wasted time fighting when I should have—I'm so sorry, Sheena. I didn't save you."

He pulled his hand away from where it had been resting on her leg. The golden cord in her chest tensed, as though the physical connection had strengthened it and now it was straining to cross the space between them.

Sheena snatched his hand back and twined her fingers between his.

"But you said it was impossible. I'm already a shifter," she said, and the words echoed in her ears.

Fleance's eyes looked haunted. "Can you find your sheep?"

She tried. God, she tried. But there was nothing inside her but emptiness... and the smell of smoke.

Her shoulders tightened. "How is that even possible? My sheep is like..." She waved her hands as though she was literally trying to pick up the words she wanted. "God, I don't know. My cousin Aroha is the one who's into all that spiritual stuff. It's a reflection of my soul and part of it, too... how can you get a new part of your soul? Or if it's a reflection of your soul, does it change who you are totally?"

She stopped. Fleance had gone gray; his face looked like a skull in the light sifting in through the window. She swallowed. "I didn't mean—obviously you didn't change who you are, when you became a hellhound shifter..."

"I don't know if you're right or not." His expression was still locked in harsh, fleshless angles, but his voice was strangely soft. Sheena pulled him closer and he moved reluctantly, as though his muscles were as paralyzed as his face. "I was eighteen when Parker turned me. I'd just lost my parents, the house I grew up in... I don't know if I am the same person I was then. Sometimes he feels like a different person."

Sheena wrapped her arms around him. "Don't say that. I'm talking rubbish, ignore me."

He shivered against her, once, then relaxed and turned towards her. He rested his head on hers and murmured, his breath rustling against her hair: "You might be right."

"I'm never right about anything," she said quickly.

"But if you are, this is the first time I've ever been truly glad Parker turned me." He lifted his head and she looked up to find him staring at her, a strange, helpless look in his eyes. "Because what I am now is your mate."

The skin around his eyes crinkled as he looked at her. Soft, gentle lines that wiped away the harder ones. Then he smiled, a crooked, tentative happiness that caught Sheena by surprise.

She touched his cheek, where the deep line on one side of his mouth had transformed into a dimple.

"If I'm your mate because of what happened then it was all worth it," he said, his voice shaking. "Becoming a hellhound. Being under Parker's control. If he'd never turned me, I wouldn't be here. I would never have met you. I'd rather be this, and yours, than anything else."

"You've only just met me," she protested. Weakly. Her heart was beating too hard for her to push away his words entirely.

"And I already know you're brave, and that you'd throw yourself into a burning building to save your family, and that… that you think things through more than you think you do." He brushed a stray strand of hair off her face and his fingers lingered along her jawline. "The mate bond is magic. It's incredible. But the fact that it means I get to know you better is the best thing about it."

Sheena had never wanted to run away more.

It was too much. She wanted to sprint as far as her legs would carry her and find a bush to crouch behind or a hole to fall down and stay hidden until she could deal with everything she was feeling. Fleance wanted to know more about her? He thought she was *brave?*

All her life she'd been treated as small and unreliable. Helpless people like her didn't need to be brave, they needed to get out of their own way and let someone else look after them.

She'd wanted to prove for so long that everyone who thought she was small and weak was wrong, but she hadn't expected it to *work*. She hadn't expected anyone to look at her and see that she was more than everyone said.

Even her mate.

To her horror, her eyes welled up.

"Don't cry," Fleance said, his own voice wavering. "The idea of me hanging around isn't that bad, is it?"

The golden thread that Sheena was still holding tight in her heart trembled. He was as scared about this as she was, she realized. The big bad wolf was as anxious to get this right as she was.

God, she didn't want to say the wrong thing and make him rethink that.

Sheena tucked herself closer against him and kissed his collarbone. His arms tightened around her. "At least we know where we stand. Together."

He lifted one of her hands and his lips grazed her knuckles. A warm hum flooded from them through the rest of Sheena's body, a long, slow uncoiling so different from other times she'd been turned on that it took her a moment to recognize. When she did, it was like opening the curtains to find the day at full light behind them. No nerves, no anxiety that she was doing the wrong thing or about to make a fool of herself—just longing and a certainty singing bright and gold inside her that that longing was returned. The only wrong note was the lump of silence deep inside her.

"Together," she said, breathing in his masculine scent. "What the hell was the universe playing at, putting us down on opposite sides of the world?"

"To hell with the universe," Fleance growled. "I found you. You're mine."

Until I turn.

Cold flooded Sheena's veins. She must have tensed; Fleance went still, his eyes locked on to her. She wet her lips and whispered the words that had appeared like spears of ice in her mind.

"It's true, isn't it? We're just waiting for it to take hold. And then he'll be able to control me like he controlled you. D-don't tell me it's not going to happen," she forced out as he opened his mouth. "I can feel it. Where my sheep used to be. There's this... bit of me, inside, that I can't see into. The edges of it hurt. They're hot. Like a cut that's got infected." She wet her lips. "Which is what it is, right? An infection."

A virus, taking over her soul and turning her into something else. Taking away a part of her she'd half-tolerated, half-resented for so long that it took her until now to realize what she really felt for it was all love.

Fleance looked as though he was struggling to stay calm. He ran one hand down his face. Fire flared in his eyes, just for a second, and he squeezed them shut. "I know!" he muttered, his voice pained, and Sheena guessed he wasn't talking to her. Her chest hurt. She'd just as good as told his hellhound it was an illness nobody wanted—which wasn't true, it was part of Fleance and Fleance was all she wanted, but if who she was changed then what she wanted would change, too...

"I should have known better than to go up against him." Fleance's voice was empty of all emotion. "I never escaped. Not truly. And now he's caught you, too."

He stood up and took a deep, shaking breath. "You're right. It's an infection. We should treat it like one. If there's any hope you can recover—" He broke off and shook his head, a short, sharp action that tugged at Sheena's heart. She knew what it meant. *Stop. Don't even think it, in case thinking it tempts fate.* "He got me in the neck and I turned quickly, but this is—it's so small an injury, maybe you can fight it off. You and your sheep together. Rest and liquids. That's what you need. We wait it out."

"No." Sheena's heart was solidly in her throat. The panic she'd felt at the first moment of realization was gone, replaced by a ferocity that barely felt like her own.

She strode over to Fleance and took his face between her hands. His skin was warm, the sandpaper of a day's stubble rough under her palms. He was tired, and in shock, and as close to falling apart as she was.

And he was *hers*.

The light inside her flared bright enough that just for a moment, she couldn't feel the numb hollow deep inside her chest. She focused on the mate bond, pouring all her new ferocity and everything else she felt into it. The joy she'd felt when she first saw him, the wonderful confusion, the way she didn't even care that they'd fallen into each other's arms in the middle of a bloody housefire and, yes, how ridiculous that was. How much more she wanted and how afraid she was of losing all those half-formed dreams.

Fleance groaned and pressed his forehead against hers. Their breath mingled as light spilled from the golden cord that connected them, overflowing with her emotions.

"You're mine," she said, her voice shaking. "And I'm yours. Now, right now, I'm *only* yours. I'm not going to sleep through what might be the only time we have together."

"But Parker—"

"If I do change, then he's going to catch up with us no matter what, right? And if I don't, we'll have to face him anyway, to stop him from hurting anyone else."

Fleance nodded reluctantly.

"I don't want to waste time running. Or *resting*. If this is the only chance we have..." She kissed him and the languid longing that had unfurled in her at his first touch quickened. Urgency crackled through her veins and when Fleance hesitated, she almost groaned aloud. Maybe it would have in different circumstances, too, but here, now, she didn't have time to think about that. She didn't want to waste another second.

She kissed him again as his fingers tightened around her waist. He kissed her back, but again, there was something missing. He was holding back.

Isn't it meant to help the mate bond form, anyway? Make it stronger? She was sure she'd heard that somewhere. Or heard gossip about it, at least. It was probably as real as anything else people said about how shifters worked. Like how—

She'd reached out to her sheep to reminisce out of habit. Her mind buffeted against the nothingness and she cringed back.

Fleance hesitated. *I want you, too.* His telepathic voice was layered over with concern, and wariness, and oh, God, yes, the same desperate need she felt. *But I don't know if this is a good idea.*

I've never had a good idea in my life. I've never let it stop me before, Sheena joked. Her telepathic voice felt raw. She wanted him so much it hurt.

She put her hands on his chest. The thin fabric smelled like washing detergent, and beneath it he smelled clean and masculine and *good.* She didn't care what he said about failing to do the right thing—he'd lost so much of his life to his evil uncle's cruelty, and if she couldn't convince him that beating himself up over not recovering as soon as he was free didn't make him a bad guy, she could at least show him it didn't change how she thought about him.

The slightest hint of smoke teased at her nostrils as she pulled him closer, but the reminder of what they'd been through just made her need him more. From the expression in his eyes, he felt the same.

He put his hands on top of hers. *I don't know how much time we have,* he admitted. His shame about not knowing enough about how the turning process worked to reassure her was clear. *I don't want to waste it, either. But I don't want to lose you because of my own selfish desires. What I want here shouldn't matter. You deserve better than—*

"Hey." She lowered her head until her lips were so close to his she could almost taste him. *What do I have to do to make it more obvious that I want this, too?*

He kissed her like a drowning man taking his first breath of air.

She had her hands on his chest. It was the perfect position to push him down onto the sofa, but she lost herself in the headrush of the kiss long enough for him to steal the lead. He picked her up, one hand around her torso and the other holding her firmly by the arse and took her to the bed.

He lay her down and kissed her until she was the one who needed to come up for air. He tugged at the hem of her shirt and she mumbled a protest.

"It's not fair," she gasped, and felt his question brush against her mind. "You kept your clothes on when you shifted before. I haven't even had a chance to perv."

Fleance barked with surprise. He buried his face in her shoulder and kissed the nape of her neck but left her shirt alone.

Sheena ran her fingers along his collar. She undid the buttons one by one, resisting the urge to kiss his chest. She wanted to see him. All of him. If this was the only time they had together, she wanted as much of him to remember as possible.

He was lean under his shirt, muscles tight and hard under her fingertips. His heartbeat thudded against her touch. Old scars crisscrossed his ribs. Sheena paused, her fingers brushing the edges of them. Shifters could scar, but it took a lot more to leave a lasting mark than it did for humans. For Fleance to have this many scars…

"Don't," he said softly. She looked up at him and he said, "I could feel you wondering. I don't want you to worry about them."

"That doesn't make it any better," she grumbled. He might not want her to worry about Parker, but she could put the dots together and figure out what he wasn't saying. Even a wooly-headed—

Cold washed over her. Was she still a wooly-headed sheep shifter? Those bursts of anger, the strange emptiness inside her—what if her sheep was gone already, forever, and she just hadn't noticed?

Fleance caught her face with one hand and turned her to look at him. *You're still you,* he sent to her, and the mate bond hummed with concern. *As long as we have this.*

Of course. She must still be wooly-headed, to forget that. The cold retreated as he kissed her and this time, she couldn't quite manage to pull away as she tugged at his jeans. The button was stiff and she almost growled against his lips as she tried to free it. As soon as it was loose Fleance shucked his jeans off and kicked them over the side of the bed. His hands were busy, stroking along her thighs and veering dangerously close to shorting out Sheena's senses entirely.

She ran her fingers under the elastic of his boxers, and he groaned. He rocked on top of her, his hips bucking as he swore under his breath, but he didn't tell her to hurry up or slow down or any of the things she could feel teetering at the edge of their connection. The hard ridge of his erection pressed against her. She could feel exactly how big he was, but her eyes still widened when she pulled his boxers off.

Whatever Fleance picked up via the mate bond made him growl and pull her close.

"Mate bond or not," he growled. "You're mine. I won't let anyone take you from me."

His breath was hot against her neck. When he kissed her, her whole body thrilled. She wanted to slow down, she wanted to speed up—she wanted everything, all at once.

"Oh…" She trailed one finger down his chest, from his collarbone to the deep v of his hip and stopped at what she hoped was an infuriatingly short distance from his cock. He moaned and sank closer against her and she relented, wrapping her fingers around his thick length. Heat pulsed between her legs.

She tipped his head back up, one finger under his chin. "Your turn."

His eyes went black with desire. "Does this mean you're done looking?"

Sheena bit her lip. "Yes?"

He pulled at her robe, unfastening the belt, peeling the fluffy fabric away inch by inch. "Then it's my turn."

This would normally be the time she got a horrible sense of self-doubt. The timing was right, and the background—she should have been writhing with embarrassment that she wouldn't live up to whatever expectations of lissome womanliness he had in his head. But she was strangely, unbelievably confident. She didn't even have a slight sense of foreboding, like she was waiting for the other shoe to drop.

She told herself it was because Fleance had already seen her naked, but that wasn't it. There hadn't been anything sexual about that.

Maybe it was something to do with the intense concentration on Fleance's face. He made her feel so special that there was no way she could disappoint him. Or—

Sheena. Fleance's voice brushed against her mind like a particularly amused breeze. *Whatever you're thinking about, stop.*

"What?"

He touched the space between her eyebrows and she realized she was frowning. She relaxed and—oh, God, at last, something normal—blushed.

"All right," she said, tripping over her words a bit, "I'll stop thinking about how amazing you are, then."

"Was that what you were thinking about, before you got distracted?"

Her blush deepened. "How do you know I was distracted?"

He didn't reply out loud, but the mate bond hummed as though someone had plucked it.

Oh, hell. This was it. The other shoe. She'd been so busy congratulating herself for not being a total dickhead that she'd fallen right into the trap of her own brain.

She had raised herself up so he could slip the robe off her shoulders; now she sank down, as quickly as her stomach was dropping.

"I really am sorry," she said, "And—I wasn't joking because I'm not taking this seriously, I was—"

She hoped he could feel the truth of that, through the mate bond. Oh, bloody hell. What else could he feel through the mate bond? If he knew how much of a fuckup she really was…

"*Stop*," he said again, and kissed her. That, finally, made her brain derail. *However briefly*, she thought, and Fleance made a noise that might have been a choked laugh. "I can see I'll have to do a better job of keeping you occupied," he said. His voice was a low growl, full of promise.

"What do you—"

He pinned her wrists to the mattress. Excitement spiked at the base of her spine. She'd felt a burst of his hunger before, but this…

He'd been holding back. For her, because she'd told him she wanted to move slowly. And now she realized that wasn't what she wanted at all.

She let go. Everything she'd been holding back, all the walls she'd built around herself. If this was the only chance they had to be each other's mates then she wanted all of him.

Fleance's pupils enlarged, until there was only a hint of sky blue around the edges of his eyes. Their darkness pulled Sheena, black fire that threatened to consume her. That she *wanted* to consume her.

He pulled her up and kissed her so passionately she lost all sense of where she was. Her head was still spinning when he moved down, hungrily laying kisses down her neck and across her breasts. He bit gently down on one nipple and she gasped. It hurt, but... good.

"Is that all right?" Fleance asked her, and she sure as hell hoped he saw her nod or felt her absolute yes telepathically, because she wasn't up to talking right now. He must have, because the next thing she felt was his voice growling *Good* into her mind and his hands on her hips.

The calluses on his fingers grazed against the soft skin on her thighs and butt as he caressed her. She moaned as he slipped one finger between her legs and found her already wet. He teased her, adding another finger as he kissed her shoulder. The slightest scrape of his teeth on her skin made her shiver.

Sheena wanted to let her eyes roll up in her head and give in, but she had to make an effort, damn it.

She wanted this to be as memorable for Fleance as it was for her.

She pushed him gently onto his back. He let her, although now that she'd felt the hunger in his mind his every movement seemed coiled with barely restrained power. It took her breath away as she straddled him and felt his strong, hard body beneath her.

His cock pressed against her inner thigh; she rubbed against it as she lowered herself over his body, making Fleance growl and send flickers of need along the mate bond. When she took it in her hand his rush of desire was so intense her own body tightened.

He was… big. She left it at that. Measurements couldn't describe the heavy weight of his cock in her hand, or the way his fingertips sank into the blankets as she stroked it. Or the way her heart leaped, half trembling and wholly excited, at the thought of taking it inside her.

A tangent threatened to open up in her mind: *He wouldn't be too big, would he? Come on. The Universe made us for each other, surely it would make sure we fit each other…*

She yanked her mind back before it could get any further—seriously, her brain needed a freaking leash sometimes—and looked up at Fleance.

If seeing the hunger in his eyes before had almost been too much for her, the expression on his face now almost broke her in a different way. His fierce, possessive passion was still there, but mingled with the vulnerability she thought she'd glimpsed when she pulled away from him in her aunts' house.

She hadn't imagined it, then. Despite his strength and power, and the action-man face he put on, he was as human as she was underneath. Or as... whatever.

The noises Fleance made—half bitten-off gasps, moans deep in his throat—as she lowered her mouth over his cock reverberated down her spine. She used her tongue, and her hands, until his hips bucked up from the bed.

She would have kept going, but his fingers grazed her shoulder and one look in his eyes told her he wouldn't be able to hold back for long.

She uncurled and kissed him, pressing her body against his. He moved against her like he knew every inch of her body already, where to touch, where to squeeze and hold. They lay side by side, facing each other. Her breath caught as she hooked one leg over his hip.

Words weren't necessary. Which was good. She didn't have any left. Just need, and desire, and the light of the mate bond coursing between them like a river of stars.

Afterwards, aching and exhausted and more dreamily content than she could ever remember being, Sheena just managed to turn the shower on and step underneath it. Sometime later, she shook herself awake, and just managed to step out of it again.

The hotel towels were huge and fluffy. She wrapped one around herself and stepped back into the bedroom.

"Are you coming to bed?" Fleance asked from the tangle of blankets she'd left him in. "Or I can take the sofa…"

A hiccup of laughter surprised her. "I think it's a bit late for that."

Her laughter turned into a slow smile that Fleance returned. Warmth rose through her body like the dawn—and dissolved just as quickly.

She didn't want to go to bed. She didn't want to go to *sleep*. She felt empty inside, lonelier than she'd ever believed possible without her sheep. Her world was crashing down around her and Fleance was the one sure thing she had left to cling to. He'd turned up out of nowhere, a magical shifter like she'd never seen before, and saved her life.

But it was more than that. The mate bond had hit her like a hammer, sure, and she'd never had sex that good before, but underneath the magic and fate and related bull, Fleance was a person. A person she *liked*. His smile, his kindness, the way he listened to her even after he found out she was a tiny sheep. The hints of softness under his strong exterior. She wanted to get to know him better, find out his habits and what he liked and didn't like, what he was like in the mornings. Whether he snored. Whether, if he snored, he was embarrassed about snoring. If he liked to have his ears scratched in hellhound form.

And she would have, if she hadn't walked straight into Angus Parker's trap.

She didn't know how much time she had, but if she got into bed now, that would be it. Hours, wasted to sleep. Her body didn't care that she wanted to stay awake. Exhaustion was already dragging at her and even keeping her eyes open was almost more effort than she could manage.

The wound in her leg ached as she put weight on it. How could it hurt more now than it had before? Fleance had told her it would leave a scar, and suddenly she was glad it would. Even though the bite was the reason everything was going wrong, it would remind her of him. The careful, tender way he'd cleaned and bound it. The touch of his fingertips on her skin. The way they'd locked eyes and she'd *known,* and had seen that same sudden wonderful understanding reflected in his face, and there was no way they weren't meant to be together because how else could you explain the way they'd both started macking on each other right then and there without stopping to think that, oh, they were in the *middle of a fire,* and it might not be the best time to act like they'd snuck behind the bike sheds. He might be a magnificent fire-breathing beast but somewhere deep inside he was as much of an idiot as she was.

Maybe if they hadn't been so perfect for one another, she wouldn't have ended up like this.

She must have tensed or sent a shiver of the hurt in her heart down the mate bond, because Fleance was suddenly alert. He half-raised himself on one elbow, his eyes glowing like cooling embers.

What's wrong?

Sheena walked over and pushed him back down, gently, and then found a place to curl herself against his side. He was warm and solid and she was going to be a goddamned grown-up about this, she told herself, and *not* cry.

"I'm scared," she admitted.

His hand swept up her side and came to rest on her shoulder. "I'm here for you, Sheena. No matter what happens." His breathing caught, then he added: "I was alone when I first changed. You won't be.

I promise. Whether it happens tomorrow or days from now, I'll be with you."

Her eyes closed. Mistake. She was still hunting for the right words to say when sleep finally took over. The last thought in her mind was, *If I wake up tomorrow and I'm part of Parker's pack...*

She put a wall around that thought and sleep dragged her down.

It wasn't words that woke her, but a feeling. Like fire kindling inside her.

She jerked awake.

Fleance was still deeply asleep, his features relaxed in a way that made Sheena suddenly realize how the deep stress lines on his forehead and around his mouth made him look so much older than he was. She froze, partly not to disturb him, partly to focus on the strange crackling under her skin.

Oh, no. Oh, no, no, no.

Heat roiled inside her. The soul-paddock where her sheep used to live churned, bubbling and writhing like a pot about to boil over.

"Oh God," Sheena gasped as it disappeared in a burst of sulfurous yellow smoke. "No!"

7

FLEANCE

Sheena's scream echoed in Fleance's dream. Then the smell of burning filled his nostrils.

That wasn't a dream.

His eyes flew open. The first thing he saw was fire. Flames poured out of the sky above him—no. Not the sky.

Sheena had fallen asleep nestled against his chest. She must have shifted before she was even awake enough to get out of bed.

Fleance sat up. There were legs in the flames, he could see that now—four legs tipped with heavy paws and, somewhere in the billowing yellow fog that smelled of brimstone and ash, a sleek body and a long head with too many teeth in it. A hellhound, wild and fierce and trapped.

He could imagine how she felt. He'd felt it himself, only a few days after his eighteenth birthday.

The mate bond was jangling with tension. But it was *there*. He wrapped his relief around it, then reached up into the inferno that Sheena was the heart of. His fingers brushed against rough fur.

Light burst above him, a shiver that made the flames look dark, and then Sheena was human again, falling into his arms.

He wrapped himself around her. She clung to him, her chest heaving, and he could just make out her words as she gasped for breath.

"You were right about—one thing," she began. "That was—I thought I was going to—"

It's fine, he was about to say—*needed* to say—*I'm with you, I promise I won't let you do this alone.*

There were tears on her cheeks. "My stupid sheep—I never thought I would miss it so much—and now—"

She pressed her head against his chest, and he braced himself for her grief to crush into him. Sharing feelings with her last night had been like bathing in sunlight; this would be like...

Ashes. Not fire, not smoke, but the gray, dead remnants of her old life. Fleance almost choked.

And then—there. A glow in the darkness. Sheena's fingernails dug into his shoulders as she held onto him, and something surged behind the mate bond.

Fleance's heart stopped. Sheena had turned. She wasn't the woman who'd fallen asleep in his arms the night before. Her hellhound was a creature of fire and smoke, terror crystallized into a shape meant to strike fear into the hindbrain of any human who set eyes on her.

And the first person it was hunting down with that fear power was Sheena herself.

He reached for the mate bond, his hellhound straining to protect her, but before he could think of how he could defend her from something that was part of herself, Sheena sat up.

Her eyes were wide. They were the same warm hazel-brown they had been when he first saw her, outlined by fire as it closed in on them both. But now the fire was inside her. She stared at him, he stared back—and something new looked out at him from her eyes. Fire and rage.

"He's coming," she whispered. Her face was pale, and despite her eyes there was no trace of hellhound in her quiet, tense voice. "I can't explain it, I just know that he knows exactly where I am, and he's coming."

Fleance remembered what that was like. How could he forget? He looked out the window, his senses straining to pick up any trace of the alpha hellhound.

Nothing. The sky was clear, a tapestry of unfamiliar stars above the city lights. It should have been reassuring, but instead a prickle of dread crept up Fleance's neck. He checked in with his hellhound, which growled unhappily.

"I believe you," he said quietly.

"We have to go!" Sheena leaped off him and dashed to his suitcase. He blinked. The air around her was smudged...

The smoke alarm on the ceiling burst into screaming life and Fleance swore. Sheena didn't react: she was busy pulling on clothes. Fleance joined her. Voices from further down the corridors filtered through the alarm's shrieks. Shouts of surprise and complaint filled the hotel.

All at once the alarm cut out and was replaced by a robotic voice telling them to leave the room and gather in the car park.

"So much for staying put," he remarked.

"We're not staying." She pulled out a shirt and tugged it on. "Forget what I said last night about not running," she said, tying her sneakers. "He's coming and when he finds me—we can't still be in the city. He'll burn it all down."

Fleance believed her. He knew what that was like: to feel his alpha's plans in his head, curdling the air he breathed. Caine kept his thoughts and his power to himself, but Parker had never seen the benefit in holding back when the alternative was putting the boot in.

"How far away is he?" he asked. "We shouldn't react without thinking. What you said last night, about doing what he expects—"

"Fleance." Sheena grabbed his arm. Her fingernails dug in, and he could feel her trembling down to her toes. "I can *hear* him. He wants the audience that he didn't get yesterday. We need to go. *Now.*"

Fleance's blood turned to ice. They were in the middle of town. It was still early enough that he couldn't hear any cars on the street outside, but all that meant was that people would be trapped in their houses if Parker tried here what he had done in Silver Springs. And that was without a carpark full of hotel guests, huddled in the dark. The perfect audience for whatever Parker had in mind.

"Where?" he asked.

Sheena shook her head, her face twisting. "I don't know! I don't know this part of the country at all. If we were back home…" She pounded the wall so hard someone yelled something, muffled, from the other side. "I know back home you couldn't go ten k' without tripping over a farmer or someone on a camping trip or bike tour. It's going to be the same here. There are too many *people*," she anguished.

"It's early," Fleance countered, "and I think our definitions of 'too many people' might be different. If we get out of the main streets—"

"*Any* is too many." She finished dressing and turned to him, her expression tortured. "He wants to hurt people, Fleance. I can feel it. I can feel what he wants to do." She ran her hands down her face.

"Maybe a national park. The tracks get closed off down south during winter. It'll be the same here, right?"

He didn't know. Worse, every time Sheena mentioned her home, the pit that had opened in his heart widened. It reminded him that strange as the geothermal land around her was to him, it wasn't her territory, either. She had a home, a life, a whole world of places and people she loved. There was so much about her that Fleance didn't know and now would never be able to learn. At least not beside her, free, souls entwined as they were meant to be.

Sheena grabbed the keys. "I don't even know how far the closest trail is. I don't know how much time we have." Her eyes blazed and she bared her teeth in an uncharacteristic growl. "He's *toying* with us."

"That sounds like him."

They raced down the stairs, past groups of confused and angry hotel guests. A security guard ushered them out through the foyer doors. There was already a small group gathered in front of the main building, but Fleance took Sheena's hand and they slipped into the shadows and headed for his car.

The early morning air was lung-tighteningly cold. Fleance worried for Sheena's bare legs until they reached his car and the ice on the door retreated at her touch. Her hand hadn't been overly hot when they were running over here—she was still volatile, this close to her first shift.

"I'll drive," he said, and her nails squealed against the metal door. She looked as though she was about to argue—then her shoulders dropped.

"Here." She tossed him the keys and slipped around to the passenger side. By the time he got the engine running, she had her seatbelt on and was sitting with her head in her hands. "I'm burning up," she whispered. "How do I control it? I can't even—I don't *want* to talk to it! I don't want this to be happening!"

He reached over and gripped her shoulder. Her skin was so hot he could feel it even through her borrowed sweater. Before he could open his mouth, she spoke again.

"But it is happening."

Her back straightened. Without thinking, as though she were a member of his pack or still his mate, Fleance sent reassurance to her—and his telepathic senses came up against a block, like a steel wall around her soul. From the set of her jaw, she hadn't even felt him reach for her.

He swallowed. "Sheena—"

"Don't." The word was almost a sob. "I know what you're trying to do. But it makes it worse, feeling you in my heart when he's—he's *watching*."

He pulled back, feeling sick.

That doesn't change anything, his hellhound hissed. He almost jumped. It had been quiet since Sheena was bitten, wary and watchful, but he'd been so focused on her that he hadn't missed it. Now it slunk around the edges of his mind, anger boiling across its hide. *We came here to make sure Parker couldn't hurt anyone else. We can't let him take her.*

His hellhound's words put iron in his spine. It was right. It was his duty to defend all of Parker's victims and make the world right.

He knew what he had to do.

Tires squealed as he pulled out of the carpark and onto the road. Someone shouted, and he felt a stab of guilt at leaving some poor fire warden short—which was ridiculous. Better their names be missing from the roster than the whole hotel be dragged into Parker's game.

Rotorua at night was eerie. The city's lights hardly made a dent in the huge blackness of the sky, and once they left streetlights behind them, the sky's emptiness came down to envelope the whole world. The stars seemed to pull back, peeling away from the earth. The car's headlights carved twin yellow beams through the nothing, illuminating roiling hisses of steam and gas and the skeletons of power lines, and nothing else.

Sheena fumbled with his phone. "Keep going," she said, thumbing through the map app. "We're on the thermal highway. That Caltex back there was the last thing we're going to hit until Tumunui, whatever that is. Wee township. Or something."

"A what?"

She looked confused. "A… small town? What would you call it?" She shook her head and flinched. Her question forgotten, Fleance clasped her hand.

"What are you getting from Parker?" he asked.

"Getting from him?"

"Distance. Direction." He tried to describe what the pack sense felt like to him.

"Like a radar?" She half-grinned, then blanched. "Oh, God. That isn't a joke. I used to be able to see my flock mentally, like someone had scattered rice on a black sheet, but…"

"I know. He's the center, and you're moving around him." He remembered it all too well: the lurch from his mental image of himself being central to his understanding of the world, to being on its periphery. From being free to being a pawn.

Sheena's voice dropped. "I might have been the smallest sheep in my flock, but at least I was still the center of my own universe." Her hands made fists on the dashboard. "Be nice if this new hellhound radar came with a scale. I can see where I am, and where he is, but not how far—"

She slammed back against the seat. Fleance didn't need to ask why. Cold fingers of dread curled around his throat. Parker was close enough that he could feel his fear magic, too. He pressed on the accelerator. The fear was coming from behind him—if he could just get enough distance—

"How is he keeping up with us? Nothing can move this fast," Sheena muttered, glancing at the speedometer. "Wait... It's a trap. It must be. He's doing the same thing he did yesterday, herding us forwards!"

"Where else are we meant to go?" The road stretched out in front and behind, empty.

Sheena pointed. Her face was skull-like, lit from below by the phone screen. "There should be a turnoff on the left before we get to Tumunui. There!"

Fleance took the turn onto a thankfully sealed road. A sign warned of logging trucks, but all that appeared in his headlights were pine trees.

Including one that had fallen to block the road.

Fleance swore and braked. He turned the car, half-expecting to find Parker looming on the road behind them. But the forest was still empty.

"There was a gravel road back there," he muttered, half to himself. "I don't know where it goes, but the more remote the better."

"Fleance..."

"Can you see on the map?"

"I..." There was a clatter and the phone fell to the floor. Its screen illuminated Sheena from below, making her face look almost skeletal. She swallowed. "Fleance, when you said hellhounds have weird powers..."

He cursed himself. He'd already seen that she was volatile—he should have seen this coming, too.

She *flickered*. Not invisibility—this was worse. Fleance gasped, despite knowing what was happening. "Try to focus on being in the car," he said, and repeated the words telepathically. Sheena's mind slid against his, one second there, the next gone. Like trying to touch mist. He went back to speaking out loud. "Don't think about stopping moving or getting out of your seat. Stay here. We're safe so long as we stick together. *Stay with me.*"

He hoped he sounded like he knew what he was talking about.

"I think it's—" She faded out again. Fleance's hand went through the space where her shoulder had been, and he snatched it back. "Afraid. Trying to get away."

"Focus," he urged her, his voice sharp with fear. Terror was building up inside him. His hellhound snapped at it. The shadowy Sheena tried to pick up the phone and it fell through her fingers. "You can turn invisible, that's fine, just don't fall out of the car."

"Oh God," she burst out. "Fall out of the car? You mean fall *through* the car? Is that even… Oh, shit, if I can walk through walls now then you're right, I could fall right through—"

"You won't." Fleance reached for her hand without taking his eyes off the road. Her hand was too warm, but it was solid. "See? You've got this. It's going to be okay. You're a, a box of birds."

Her fingers tightened around his and she snorted. Fleance was about the reach for the mate bond, hoping to find her smirk reflected there, but remembered just in time.

He swallowed.

Outside, the world was blanketed in white. Frost glittered in the headlights, and the trees on the side of the road clutched frozen lumps of snow in their branches. He thought of something that might reassure her.

"I know it seems bad now, but we're going to get through this," he said, scoping out the road ahead. Sheena had mentioned national parks might be an option to avoid any collateral damage; this forest might not be a real park, but it was isolated enough. "If there's anything I've learned these past few years, it's always worth holding out for a Christmas miracle."

"That's… a long wait." Sheena sounded baffled.

Fleance frowned. Winter had the world firmly in its grip; true, he hadn't seen festive decorations other than posters advertising a light show and banners with stars on them, but he knew in a vague sort of way that not all countries went as full-tilt into Christmas celebrations as America did. He said as much to Sheena.

"Those are Matariki decorations," she said. "For when the constellation reappears in the sky. Christmas isn't until summer."

The world tilted around Fleance. He *knew* the seasons were reversed south of the equator. But he'd known it with his head, not his heart, and it was his heart that had clung to the cold and the dark as signs that things would end up okay.

"Forget I said anything," he muttered.

Sheena's eyes narrowed. *Did someone just laugh?* Her voice brushed against his mind, but it felt undirected, as though she was poking around randomly.

"Invisible…" She looked up at the rear-view mirror just as the car went over a bump in the road. The seatbelt rattled tight, snapping through her chest to lie flush against the seat behind her. Sheena's eyes went wide. She flickered out of sight and Fleance hit the brakes. If she'd phased through the car—

Then she popped back into sight. Screaming.

"He's in the car," she yelled, *Run, get out, he's already here!*

8

SHEENA

It was a trap. Sheena's throat closed over as surely as if the man looming in the back seat of the car had put his fingers around it.

She'd never seen Parker's human form before, but there was no question who he was. He looked like he was in his fifties or early sixties: sleek, too-shiny face, hair too solidly colored to be real. Like a door-to-door salesman who keeps bodies in the back of his car, she thought. He smiled when he saw her looking at him, and the expression was all predator.

Time slowed down. She'd thought he was herding them, but that must have been a distraction. He'd been there all along.

He must have been waiting all night, she thought, cold tendrils snaking around her stomach. *He must have known we would try to flee as soon as I turned.*

All he needed to do was phase into the car and wait.

Parker leaned forward and fire roared up inside her, sudden and terrifying. *No!* a voice roared in her head, familiar and strange at the same time.

Fleance shouted something. She saw, and felt, him reaching for her, body and mind turning towards her as his mouth moved voicelessly. Something inside her reached for him as well.

And stopped. Sheena felt dizzy. Her hellhound was a strange, wary thing. It felt more like a collection of instincts than an animal. Fear. Hatred. So much hatred, of the dark star that had formed in the center of her heart and kept trying to draw her closer. The cold, disgusting counterpart of the light that was her connection to Fleance.

Her hellhound saw the light of the mate bond and *screamed*. It didn't see *him*; it saw a way away from Parker's web. But if she reached out to Fleance, that would only draw him closer to Parker again. To the life he'd suffered under for so long.

She had to let him go. If there was some way of breaking the mate bond—

NO!

She dropped through the bottom of the car like a stone. It spun away as she hit gravel, rolling to a stop at the side of the road. Bracken crunched beneath her as she stood up on all four legs.

Her eyes were fire, her lungs were fire, fire filled the pit of her stomach and roared in her veins. She was a hellhound, burning with her first breaths. Ahead, the car spun to a stop. The scents of the men inside filtered to her, muddied by the smell of hot rubber and burning fuel. Her alpha, the central point around which her world rotated, and her mate.

Her mate, who was trapped because of her. Parker's alpha control over her, her mate bond to Fleance. One long leash.

The ground rocked under her paws. *I can't let this happen.*

The part of Sheena that was Sheena and the part of her that was a hellhound tore apart. She felt lost and hopeless, more alone than she'd ever been in her life.

Something deep inside her growled.

The car burst open. No—two hellhounds burst *through* it. Fleance smashed his way out through the front, shredding the metal door as though it was tissue paper, but the alpha hellhound simply stood up through the roof and jumped casually to the ground. Sheena tensed, expecting the gravel to hiss and spit beneath his paws, but he wasn't setting anything on fire.

Yet.

Well now, that wasn't too bad for a first attempt! Parker's wolfish grin made Sheena's hackles rise. *You should have seen how long it took my boy there to figure out how this shit works when he first shifted.*

Don't talk about him like that! she snarled back, and then blinked. *She* snarled? She never snarled. But when she thought about what Fleance had told her about how Parker had treated him, her ears flattened against her head. It must be the new shape doing it, she thought. Fangs and claws had to be used for something, after all.

Parker's eyes blazed. Something wriggled inside Sheena's head like she'd just opened an old takeaway container and found it full of maggots. Part of her wanted to run—not a very fangs-and-claws part, true—but how could she run away from what was inside her own head?

Now you're starting to understand. Parker stretched out his neck and the maggots in Sheena's head writhed in time with his voice. No, not in time with it—they *were* his voice. Wrongness crashed through her. Speaking telepathically was like brushing up against someone else's mind, but Parker's voice wormed its way up from *inside* her.

Fleance had told her about this. She'd known it was awful, but now that she was experiencing it herself, she wanted to take him away and keep him somewhere no one could do this to him again.

Parker laughed. *Not much of a one for self-preservation, are you? You know I gotta admit, I didn't know if this was going to work. That's why I targeted the other ladies. Just to test the waters, you know? Birds, sheep, nothing I couldn't clean up easy if things didn't work out as planned.*

Clean up? Sheena's stomach dropped. Fleance had said Parker never killed, but that had been when he had Fleance to do his dirty work. Sheena couldn't believe that Fleance had never fought his alpha's command. And he might say now that he would murder Parker, but it was obvious how difficult he found the idea. She would bet that Parker had known he could only push Fleance so far. The whole alpha control thing couldn't be unbreakable.

Which meant they might have a way out of this without her mate turning into a murderer.

And isn't that a tragedy, Parker's voice drawled in her head, like oil and nails. Sheena stomach went cold.

She was trapped. She knew that. And Parker was inside her head. The thoughts jolted around her mind, too frantic to come together and make any sort of conclusion. She was fire and rage and teeth and claws and a cringing, writhing fear that she'd never experienced when she had her sheep. A fear that made all the rest of it worthless. What was the use of all this strength if she was too afraid to use it against the one creature she wanted to take down?

Parker winked at her, and the sight of one burning eye closing and opening was somehow more horrifying than anything else. Maybe because it was so human, she thought, her mind bouncing off on a tangent that she really didn't have time for.

Doing what I do best, Sheena thought to herself, not thinking about how she'd normally think it to her sheep and launched herself down the tangent. Hellhounds were the sort of overwhelmingly terrifying that ranked on a scale alongside earthquakes and tsunamis. Scary, but inevitable, and simple in their inevitability. Burny dog makes things burn. Scary magic makes things scared. But that wink was entirely human and human evil was far more complex than natural disasters.

Parker yawned. *All this and we haven't said hello yet? You'll give me a big head.*

And he could read her mind.

Quick on the uptake, aren't ya?

She wasn't even sure she could read her own mind, most of the time. Another tangent appeared. Sheena shot towards it like a dog towards its bowl. This *was* what she did best and right now, it might be her only chance, a thought she veered away from like it stung. Luckily, she always had another useless thought to grab onto, something only vaguely related to the topic at hand, like—What's the time, Mr. Wolf…

Enough. Parker was losing patience. His emotions lashed through the writing surface of his psychic presence in her mind. He stepped forward, all arrogant confidence, blocking Sheena's half-view of the movement behind him she'd been so careful to ignore.

This whole exchange had taken less than the time it took her to catch her breath. Enough time to—

She stopped thinking about that, just in time for the maggots in her head to tighten. The thought-tangent slammed shut.

There. Was that so hard? Parker's voice was layered over with greasy smoothness. *Pay attention. You might have been livestock before, but you're mine now. One of the family. And the first step in our on-boarding process—*

Sheena was trying not to see, but her skin prickled with anticipation for the thing she was trying not to think about, either. Wriggling around in her mind, feeding off her thoughts, Parker didn't need any more warning than that.

He spun around.

Fleance was standing on the wreck of the car. Parker had turned around just as he was preparing to attack, but when he saw he'd been spotted, Fleance stilled.

Did you really think that would work? Parker sounded scornful. *I would have thought you'd know better than to attack me now.*

Fleance glowered at him. If Sheena didn't know they were both the same type of shifter, she would have thought Fleance was some sort of magical fire creature, and Parker was a demon. They were both black dogs the size of no fucking dog she'd ever seen, but while Fleance's coat looked like someone had combed the night sky, Parker's was ragged, with raw-looking skin showing through the gaps. Smoke curled from his skin like steam from Rotorua's earth. She'd thought she was imagining it last time, or mixing it up with the smoke from the burning houses, but now...

Fleance bared his teeth in a snarl. *I've had enough of your games, Angus. You can't keep treating people like pawns!*

Why not? Parker yawned. *No one's stopped me yet.*

Caine did. And by the look of you, it almost killed you.

Anger writhed in Sheena's head. She was on her feet and growling before she realized it wasn't *her* anger. She cowered backwards, hoping Fleance hadn't seen her reaction.

Fleance seemed completely focused on Parker. He either didn't care about, or couldn't feel, the anger seeping as thick as oil from the alpha hellhound's mind.

I came here to make you pay for what you did, Angus. You hurt so many people and used us to do it. Manu, Rhys and me—we were just kids! I'd just lost my parents. I trusted you. How could you do this to me?

Parker sighed and flicked his ears. His emotions rolled over Sheena, thick and foul. He didn't even *care.* He was happy to let the kid whine, let him get it out, but—

Sheena was as off-guard as Parker was when Fleance struck.

He didn't stop talking, or rear up, or tense. He had no tell at all. One second, he was standing on the ruined car and Sheena was trying desperately not to let Parker's description of his voice as *whining* taint her own mind, and the next he was in the air. Parker jerked into motion, but he wasn't quick enough. Fleance hit him and they both went down in a roar of sulfurous smoke.

9

FLEANCE

He couldn't believe it had worked.

He knew what Parker thought of him. That he was a shrinking coward, too pathetic to realize how useless it was to fight against Parker's chains. The fight the day before would have proved to Parker that he was still too weak-spined to stand up for himself. That he wouldn't take Parker down if it meant risking inviting him back inside his head.

That was then. Now, he had Sheena to protect. Anything was worth keeping her safe.

So, he'd whined, and complained, his voice as nasal and annoying as he could make it without taking the piss. And when he'd seen Parker relax and—heart sinking—Sheena let down her guard, he'd made his move. Halfway through a sentence, mid-complaint. Bam.

And now he had Parker in the dirt.

The larger hellhound scrabbled at the ground, trying to get enough purchase to pull himself upright. Fleance didn't let him. He pinned Parker with his forelegs, snapping at his shoulder and neck.

Parker snarled at him, foul-smelling saliva dangling from his jaws. He surged forward and Fleance just managed to dodge his teeth. The movement put him off-balance and Parker took advantage at once, slithering to his feet.

He didn't stop. Neither did Fleance. By the time Parker had put on an unnatural burst of speed and slithered to where he was, he'd already dodged aside in time to rake his claws down Parker's flank. Parker screamed and turned on him. They faced off, stalking around one another, each waiting for the other to make a mistake.

They both made the same one.

Sheena came out of nowhere. She attacked Parker from behind, giving Fleance the opening he needed.

They circled him like sharks. Fleance tried not to be distracted by the way Sheena stalked—her pure, animal grace. When he snapped at Parker, she charged him; when he wheeled around, she was already there. Even without the mate bond, they moved in unnatural harmony.

But every movement cost Sheena, more and more. Her feet twitched as she set them down, trying to force her onto another course. By the time they managed to pin Parker down, she was panting, short, pained gasps.

This close, Fleance could smell the rot in his uncle's flesh. Something was wrong with him. More wrong than usual. It was as though the evil in his soul had started affecting him physically, as well.

Parker's head was hard against the ground. His one visible eye rolled to fix on Fleance.

Checkmate, his uncle hissed.

No. Flames licked at the corners of Fleance's mouth. *You made a mistake, uncle. You shouldn't have touched Sheena. You could have walked away, and none of this would be happening.*

Walk away? Parker was all fire and sick-smelling yellow smoke. *Walk away? Look at me!*

I'm looking. What happened, your Portrait of Dorian Gray finally overloaded?

I'm an ALPHA. I need a pack! You think I'd let an opportunity like her just walk away? Beside Fleance, Sheena whined. He moved his weight so she could lean on him, but she stayed away, trembling.

He had to finish this. Everything Parker was feeling would be boiling through Sheena's brain. She was strong, but he wouldn't put her through a second more of that torture than was necessary.

This is meant to be the lucky country, Parker raged. *My luck! Mine for the taking!*

The lucky country? That's Australia, Sheena murmured. *Dick.*

His eye rolled towards her and she flinched before he glared up at Fleance again. *Now,* he said, his voice bubbling with hatred.

Now?

No! I won't!

Sheena's voice crashed through his head. She cringed back and Parker slid away, insubstantial as smoke.

Keeping one eye on the other hellhound, Fleance turned to Sheena. *What's wrong?*

Her eyes were wide with panic. He took a step closer to her and she snapped at him. If he hadn't jumped back, she would have bitten his face.

No! she cried again, stumbling backwards on feet that seemed to be trying to stay locked in place. *Stop it!*

I'm not going to sugarcoat it, kid. You should have seen this coming. I would have turned her even if she wasn't your special girl, but now?

Parker's voice slithered against his mind. Fleance's skin crawled. Caine described Parker's mental presence as like chains, but Fleance had always felt it as vines, or tentacles, creeping *Alien*-like into his soul. He told himself that Parker couldn't reach him now—his voice was slithering *against* his mind, not into it—but it didn't stop his hellhound scratching the ground. He wasn't sure whether it was trying to run at Parker or dig through the earth to escape him.

He couldn't let that happen to Sheena. It had taken Parker weeks to break him; he hadn't even managed to hold Caine for a day.

You know the difference between you and me, Flea? I've got it figured out. I've got a growth mindset. His voice was a hiss, searching for a gap in his mental defenses. *I've learned from my mistakes.*

What was he talking about? What did *Parker* have to figure out? Fleance's hellhound growled fire as he turned his focus inwards, bulwarking the shields around his mind until there was no way Parker could get in.

His shields hummed as Parker said something, but they were so thick not even his words could make it through. He didn't need telepathy to know the bastard was laughing.

He'd already wasted too much time.

Fleance twisted all of his hellhound's rage and strength together, honing it sharp as a knife. It was almost enough to make him forget the blood trickling down his leg. The way he wasn't putting all his weight on it, because he wasn't sure it would take it.

He would get one chance to strike—just one. And the trick he'd tried before wouldn't work. This time there would be no surprises. Just strength against strength, and he had to hope the hits he'd managed to land on Parker already would even the field.

He charged forward.

Straight into Sheena.

She'd come out of nowhere, and the noise she made as he struck her took all the breath out of his lungs. He staggered back. *Sheena—what are you doing?*

Her lips twisted back over her teeth and the skin on her shoulders twitched as though she was in pain.

I can't stop it, she growled. *Fleance—*

Her voice cut off with a yelp. Fleance snarled defiance at his uncle.

Leave her out of this!

She got herself involved, Parker sneered. *Hitting me with that plank—she'll pay for that. Oh, don't worry, kid, I'm not going to hurt her.* he drawled before Fleance could respond. *You know me better than that. I'm not going to touch the girl. Hell, you're doing a good enough job of that yourself. Me? I'm giving her a job. A future.*

As your hitman.

Sheena was still standing like a statue. Her legs quivered under a too-familiar strain. Fleance didn't need to imagine what she was feeling; he'd experienced it too many times himself.

Parker laughed in his face. *Hitman? You've been watching too many movies. Try a couple of legal dramas, instead. You think I'd go to all this trouble to get done for murder?* He pushed on his powers, giving the impression of looming forward without actually moving an inch. Fleance's hellhound scratched the ground. It had to be his imagination, but he thought the ground rumbled in response.

Parker's voice wormed back into his head. *Murder leaves bodies. You know how I feel about mess, kid. It's just not me! Look, what we had before worked, and I don't see any reason to fix something that ain't broken. It'll be just like the good old days. Me sweet-talking the clients, and the young lady on hand for... negotiations.*

That would have been enough to make Fleance leap on him, but despite his lazy drawl Parker's eyes were sharp. And Sheena was still between them. A human shield. Fleance wasn't willing to bet her safety on his ability to move faster than Parker could order her to get in his way.

He forced himself to relax. If Parker made a surprise attack, he didn't want to be paralyzed in place. *Especially if he makes Sheena do it*, he thought, and felt sick.

How is this learning from your mistakes? It's the same thing you did with Manu, Rhys and me. How did that work out again? he said to Parker, hoping his voice didn't betray just how scared he was. He didn't see any way out of this except by taking down Parker—and that meant going through Sheena. Could he do that? Even to save her?

Well, on a smaller scale, to start with. Don't want to push her in at the deep end, Parker joked, as Sheena's sides trembled with stifled movement. Her back twitched as though her own muscles were fighting against her attempts to escape the alpha's control. *Unless...*

Fleance's attention snapped back to him. *Unless what?*

If there was any way to get Sheena out of this, he would take it.

Parker scraped one forepaw casually against the gravel. *Training up new hires is no one's idea of a good time. Remember how long it took with the brown fella? It's gotta be something in the water down here. If it's going to take as long with your girl—*

Dread clawed its way up Fleance's spine.

—maybe we can come to an arrangement that benefits us both.

What do you mean? Fleance snarled.

I need a crew. You need your mate to keep her hands clean. Parker's grin became feral. *Your new alpha obviously doesn't give a shit about you leaving the pack. Come back to your old job and I won't need to waste time getting your replacement up to speed.*

Fleance's hellhound stilled. The air around him went clammy, as though the ice on the ground was rising to cling to his coat, seep in deep to curl around his bones. Parker thought Sheena was still his mate.

That made her the best piece of leverage he could have.

Don't do it! Sheena's voice knifed into his mind, ragged-edged and desperate. *It's not w—*

Her voice cut off and she flinched, her whole body clenching into a fist. Fleance's hellhound snarled. How dare Parker do this to her!

When he spoke again, Parker's voice was lazy, as though he wasn't tightening his grip on Sheena's chains.

What do you say, kiddo? Things always worked smoothest when it was just the two of us, anyway.

Because after Parker had turned Rhys and Manu, Fleance hadn't been able to ignore his true feelings about what Parker was making him do.

We'll make it a proper family business again. Parker chuckled. *Whaddaya say?*

Don't listen to— Sheena's voice cut off again, as though a door had slammed shut in her face.

Fleance's heart hurt, somewhere in the dulled, numb mass of his body. Sheena knew what being under his uncle's control meant, and she still wanted him to save himself.

He couldn't do it. He hadn't been able to save Sheena before, and he couldn't defeat Parker in combat, that much was clear. He wasn't an alpha. He wasn't strong enough. The only way he could protect Sheena now was to agree to Parker's terms.

You should be jumping for an opportunity like this, Parker said. *Don't wait around, I might change my mind.*

Fleance lowered his head. His hellhound snarled, even though the gesture wasn't one either hound would recognize as submission.

And it wasn't. He was stalling for time. He had to think of something. *Anything.*

The thought of leaving Sheena to her fate didn't cross his mind. Mate or not, his or not, he couldn't do that to her.

Fleance reached out to her, trying to touch her mind and send her some reassurance, however ringed around with fear and anger, that he knew what she was going through and wouldn't let Parker get away with it—but he couldn't.

Instead of her mind, the hop-skip of energy and sunlight warmth that had so quickly become as familiar to him as his own face, he found roiling clouds of smoke. Black and thick, swirling around a center so dark that if he didn't already know Sheena, he would be afraid of what it hid.

This was what it meant to be a hellhound. Until she learned to control the maelstrom inside her, even humans would feel on edge around her. Shifters would run screaming. Who wouldn't, faced with something like that?

Fear streaked like lightning through the clouds surrounding Sheena's mind. Fleance's heart beat faster as they touched against him. It was pure adrenal reaction, on her part as much as his. The same burst of panic that had escaped him when he first set eyes on her.

And she hadn't run.

He'd never had a chance to save any of the others. But this was his chance to save her.

Time's a wasting, kiddo. Parker's spine clacked as he stretched. He wasn't even putting on an act of staying alert now; it was obvious that Fleance wasn't a threat. *Do we have a deal?*

He wasn't. Exhausted and bleeding, heartsick and desperate, Fleance knew it was true.

A shiver shuddered through him. *No way out.* Just like before. All those long years of trying to hold onto some core sense of self as Parker's control eroded everything else about him.

And Manu. And Rhys.

He raised his head.

Deal.

10

SHEENA

Sheena's ears roared as Fleance agreed to Parker's deal. He was going to do it. Give up the freedom he'd only just begun to believe could be his... for her.

She'd tried to tell him it wasn't worth it. From what he'd told her, he'd been through hell as part of Parker's pack. Wasn't that what had brought him here: his hellhound's need to replenish his soul by righting what Parker had put wrong?

And now he was going to be back where he started. Because of her. Because she'd been too daft to get out of the way of Parker's hellhound when even an actual sheep would have known he was bad news. Because her sheep—her throat constricted with grief—her sheep had always believed everything would turn out all right. Well, it bloody well hadn't this time, had it? The one silver lining was that she was evidently as shit a hellhound as she was a sheep. If Fleance had just not been the total goddamn good guy that he was and agreed to take the fall for her, she probably would have brought Parker down from the inside through sheer incompetence. But he hadn't, because he was good, and brave, and Parker had slammed the gate on her telepathic abilities before she could convince him to save himself.

Move.

She barely registered Parker's voice before her legs responded to his order. She skittered sideways, legs moving out of tandem with one another, and almost fell over. Parker ignored her as he stalked over to Fleance, who was trembling with barely controlled despair.

She tried to reach out to speak to him again. Reassure him. Anything. It was no use. Parker wouldn't let her anywhere except inside her own head. A head that hardly felt like hers, anymore. The crystalline terror she'd felt when she first sensed Parker's presence had clouded over, full of smoke and hot ash. It was almost as though the smoke was trying to hide her thoughts from Parker.

Well, good luck with that. From what Fleance had said it was a pointless endeavor.

She drew a ragged breath that almost choked her. Everything had gone wrong and Fleance was going to pay the price.

What a load of bullshit. The words thundered through her head. Not Parker's, not Fleance's—not from outside of herself. Whatever her *self* was now.

As usual her first thought was that they were Aroha's words, Aroha's voice, but they weren't. And they couldn't be her hellhound's. It wasn't a creature that had words, yet.

Hope sparked inside her. Could it be her sheep? It had been so silent she'd thought it was gone forever, but maybe—no. Her sheep was many things but she wasn't sure it even knew what swearing *was*.

That only left one option.

The voice… was hers.

She wasn't used to her voice *thundering*. Not in her head, not anywhere. Or sounding so confident.

But it—*she*—was right, wasn't she? This whole thing was bullshit. Parker, packs, alphas being supposedly so much more important than everyone else—it was all a bloody con.

Something rose up inside her like a pot boiling over. It was the smell of smoke in the dark night, harsh and bitter on the back of her tongue, but it was more than that. Lanolin. Sweet clover. The restlessness of dry grass tickling the backs of her knees, combined with and at odds with a deep and unyielding focus. It filled her from heart to fingertips, driving away the rancid maggot-touch of Parker's power.

Parker's snout whipped around, teeth bared. *What was that?*

Sheena didn't reply. Not because she didn't know the answer—well, maybe a bit—but mostly because the bitter-clover-sweet boiling inside her was expanding past her skin now. It crept out in bursts and sparks. It should have looked like whatever was happening to Parker, like her skin was splitting apart, but instead it felt...

She looked past Parker and met Fleance's gaze. The air between them crackled.

The hell with Parker, and packs, and alphas, and all the shifter mythos she'd spent her life happily not knowing.

Fleance was *hers*, and she wasn't going to let anyone take him away from her.

HIM, her inner animal roared inside her head. Thunder? This was the whole storm. *HE TRIED TO TAKE OUR MATE FROM US!*

She glared down at Parker. *Down?* she thought, *How am I looking* down *at him?*

That one moment of distraction was just enough for her inner animal to take control.

It lunged forward, fire streaming from its nostrils. Parker lurched away and Sheena's hooves cut into the gravel where he'd been. Her teeth snapped together a hand's breadth from his tail.

What? Parker's eyes narrowed and his power tightened around Sheena's limbs. At least it tried to.

Her animal sneered and shook it off. *How is this possible?*

How is *it possible?* Sheena wondered, as amazed as he was.

Fleance's voice flickered against her mind, hushed and rough-edged but wonderful. *Sheena, you're…*

Enough! Parker raged. *What is this? Some kind of trick?* His power twisted around Sheena again. This time she barely needed to shrug to get rid of it. *What are you?*

What you made me, she reminded him. But that couldn't be entirely true, because she wasn't tripping over her feet anymore. And she'd landed on *hooves*, not paws…

Parker's lip curled. *I had nothing to do with this… this… monstrosity!*

You're one to talk, she retorted, *you mangy, moth-eaten dishrag! I'm—*

She stopped. What was she? Not a sheep anymore. Surely. A hellhound? But she was looking *down* on Parker now, not up like she had when she was a sheep *or* a hellhound. But she still felt all brimstone-fiery—but…

You're incredible. Fleance's voice stopped her runaway train of thought. *Look.*

He sidestepped to the edge of one of the still pools. Keeping one wary eye on Parker, who was still muttering to himself, Sheena followed him.

Untold years of silica had built up around the pool's edges in a vibrant orange, but the water itself was crystal clear. Sheena checked Parker's position again—Fleance was standing protectively between her and the other hellhound, but his sides were still heaving as he obviously tried to ignore his injuries—and looked down into the water.

She had no idea what she was looking at.

HA HA, said the storm inside her head. *JUST AS I EXPECTED!*

So, what exactly is it I'm looking at, Sheena asked it before her silence could stretch out too long.

DON'T YOU RECOGNIZE ME? IT'S ME! AT LAST! The reflection puffed up. *MY TRUE, INNER, MAGNIFICENT SELF!*

Sheena's eyes widened. Internally. The glowing pits in the reflection stayed shiny—and burning—with smug glee.

Her inner self? Beneath the thunder and lightning, the animal did sound like… her sheep. And…

She looked closer at the reflection in the pool.

Beneath the flames spouting from her mouth and nostrils, behind the eyes like twin pits to Hell itself and under the dark smoke that coiled from her coat like she was smuggling dry ice…

A big-eyed face covered in curly black hair. Two soft ears and two curling dark horns twisting over where her hair turned white on the rest of her head and body.

Her sheep, but massive. Still adorable, also on fire. Not a hellhound, a… hellsheep?

HELLSHEEP! YES! THAT'S ME!

You're very loud, Sheena thought at it, feeling ever so slightly overwhelmed.

GOOD!

Having fun ogling yourself in the mirror, Snow White? Parker sneered. *That's enough. You're still mine. Whatever you are.* His voice prickled with opportunity. *A hellhound-sheep hybrid? Looks like I can turn other shifters after all. Now that's interesting. If I can do the same to other shifters… Might end up a bit of a menagerie but hell, everyone's banging on about diversity these days…*

The hellsheep snorted out brimstoney smoke. *HE'S RIGHT. ENOUGH! WE SHALL END THIS!*

Parker's voice wormed around her legs like slithering chains. *Trot on over here, girlie.*

You said you would let her go! Fleance growled.

His uncle blinked at him, slow and condescending. *If you'll recall, kiddo, I said I wouldn't make her work jobs for me. Let her go? Are you kidding me? I mean, sure, those teeth don't look any good for biting unreasonable clients, but she can still make herself useful doing the coffee.*

Fleance bristled, but it was Sheena who lunged forwards, her hellsheep's voice roaring in her skull: *TEETH? I'LL SHOW YOU TEETH!*

There was a brief psychic pinch as Parker, rearing up, tried to pin her in place with his alpha powers, but the cables around her legs snapped like daisy-chains. He almost fell over backwards in surprise as the hellsheep bore down on him.

At the last second, his eyes flashed with alarm—quickly covered over by a sneer of disdain. The smoke seeping from beneath his fur thickened at the same time the fur itself faded away. In less than the time it took Sheena to leap at him, he'd faded completely from view. There was nothing but a wisp of smoke in the air.

The hellsheep's teeth clacked shut in the air where Parker had been a moment before. *COWARD!* it roared. *COME OUT AND FIGHT!*

He'd turned invisible, Sheena thought, then added: But if he was *just* invisible, her teeth would have chomped *something.* Which meant he wasn't just invisible, he must be...

Like when I fell through the car, Sheena thought, and concentrated.

Fleance's voice brushed against her mind. *He's phased out. But since you're his pack, you should be able to match his... Rhys calls it a frequency. We could all do *it. But we could never use it to fight him. If you can shake off his chains like that…**

HE'LL NEVER KNOW WHAT'S COMING! Sheena's hellsheep trumpeted.

Might as well give it a go, Sheena added. Fleance wouldn't have heard her hellsheep, but he heard her. His body radiated worry.

Be careful.

I will, she reassured him.

GET READY TO DIE, ARSEHOLE! roared her hellsheep, and she added silently: *Of course, I'm not sure I'm the one who gets to decide whether I'm careful or not…*

All it took was the memory of the car seat turning to mist beneath her, and she was there. The closest thing she could compare it to was trying to open her eyes in a dream. The world around her looked convincing enough, but part of her brain still thought she was asleep.

Her hellhound stepped forward. Its leg passed through a small shrub like it wasn't there. *Feels like a dream,* she thought, dazed. Then: *If I can walk through things that are* on *the ground, then does that mean I could fall* through *the ground…*

STOP THINKING, her hellsheep demanded. *START DOING!*

She couldn't see Parker, but she didn't need to see him. Her brain felt like it was short-circuiting, a runaway train rebuilding the track underneath itself. She couldn't see Parker but she could *feel* where he was. That radar in her head dealt to that.

Her hellhound bounded forward. It moved like a rugby ball: quickly and unexpectedly. Sheena homed in on what the radar map in her mind told her should be the center of her universe. Her hooves flickered through spindly trees and hardy fences, across ground sizzling beneath the frost and over vents hissing with steam. She didn't know how far she ran, only that the air was growing paler around her and the bastard in her sights could run as fast as she could.

Almost.

A surge of energy drove Sheena forwards. She laughed deliriously. The air was thick with steam, now, and running through it—*through* through, not even touching it—felt like some wicked, daring trespass. Which it was. She'd passed a stay-on-the-path sign a ways back—passed *through* it as she nipped at Parker's tail—and she was far, far off the trail now.

Mud boiled at her feet. The sky was wide and open above her, the blaze of stars a scream in the darkness that tore at her own heart. She wanted to sprint into the sky and tear the stars out by their roots and eat them, just because she wasn't meant to.

She felt more alive than she ever had before. She felt... *right.*

OF COURSE YOU FEEL RIGHT! Her hellsheep bellowed. *DO YOU KNOW HOW LONG I'VE WANTED TO DO THIS?*

Sheena understood at once. Ignore instructions? Wander off-track? Her sheep had spent its whole life acting like it was indestructible.

Now, for the first time, it was.

Or near enough, she added, and her hellsheep sent a derisive snort of brimstone-etched smoke across her thoughts.

NEAR ENOUGH? PAH! WE'LL SEE ABOUT THAT! The hellsheep stamped its hooves in the dirt. Parker wheeled around. For a moment, Sheena thought he was about to attack. Despite her hellsheep's confidence, her heart fluttered. She couldn't help remembering the last time they had fought. Parker had moved so quickly she had no chance to get out of his reach.

NOTHING WILL EVER DO SOMETHING LIKE THAT TO US AGAIN, her hellsheep growled. *ESPECIALLY NOT SOME PUNY, STINKY DOG.*

Parker bared his teeth. *You've made your point.*

Have I? Sheena wondered. She'd just been chasing him. It wasn't exactly a cogent argument.

What was she going to do next?

PUSH HIM INTO A MUD PIT, her hellsheep suggested. *SEE HOW HE LIKES IT!*

Us falling into that hole wasn't anything to do with him, Sheena reminded it, but the hellsheep didn't care.

YOU'RE STILL AFRAID, it boomed. *THIS IS WHAT HE DOES—SCARES PEOPLE. HURTS PEOPLE. OR MAKES THEM SO SCARED THEY HURT THEMSELVES AND BLAME THEMSELVES FOR IT.*

There was the tiniest, thinnest sliver of shame hiding in its voice. It had been scared, too, Sheena realized. Parker's fear magic hadn't touched it, but the sensation of losing itself, becoming something else—no wonder it had hidden itself away.

You always tried to protect me, Sheena thought wonderingly. *Whenever I was scared, or worried, you'd make us run off away from whatever it was. I thought it was annoying, but you were only trying to help.*

DON'T NEED TO RUN AWAY NOW, her hellsheep boomed, its voice slightly bashful.

No, Sheena agreed. *I'm sorry I didn't understand when you were trying to protect me. And I'm sorry I didn't tell you how much you meant to me before Parker bit us.*

WE CAN TALK ABOUT THAT LATER, her hellsheep said quickly. *OR NOT AT ALL.*

Sheena laughed. Of course her hellsheep was allergic to talking about feelings.

All right then, she told it. *Let's deal with this arsehole first. We can't let him hurt anyone else.*

BOIL HIM IN A MUD PIT, her hellsheep suggested.

Um…

Fleance appeared at the edge of her vision, slinking like a black shadow around the edge of the thermal clearing. Certainty settled in Sheena's stomach. With her hellsheep on attack and Fleance on defense, there was no way Parker was getting away.

What did you want to do with this guy, again? she asked Fleance.

Make him pay. His voice was just as she remembered it from the first time they met: hard and determined. But there was a thread of uncertainty, like a fracture in a rock.

Sheena told him about her hellsheep's suggestion.

No. To her surprise, she could hear an echo of his hellhound in his voice, like logs spitting on a fire. But it wasn't arguing with his 'No,' like her hellsheep would have. Instead, it lent his voice a sense of righteous gravity.

There was a pause, as though Fleance was discussing something with his inner animal. **Penance,** he said at last. **That's what my hellhound wants. Not revenge. It wants Parker to make right everything he's done wrong.**

He's hurt so many people, Sheena replied. *Where's he going to start?*

Right here. Fleance let Parker hear him this time. *He can start by rebuilding Silver Springs.*

I can what? Parker snorted.

How are we going to make him do that? Sheena wondered out loud. THREATEN HIM WITH THE MUD PIT, her hellsheep suggested. There aren't any mud pits there, Sheena reminded it, it's not MUD Springs…

IRRELEVANT, her hellsheep retorted. WE'LL TAKE ONE OF THESE ONES.

What do you mean, 'take'? That's not how mud pools work! It'll get cold!

WE CAN HEAT IT UP AGAIN. Her hellsheep sounded annoyed. THAT'S HOW FIRE WORKS. MAYBE ONE OF FLEANCE'S DRAGON FRIENDS COULD HELP US.

Do I need to remind you I'm an alpha? Parker snarled. *How do you plan to make me do anything?*

He has a point, Fleance muttered.

No, he doesn't! What does being an alpha have to do with it? He's only one shifter. There's two of us!

You still don't get it, do you? Honestly, I knew this place was a backwater but I thought you'd know something about how shifters work. Parker stood taller, his eyes glowing. *Alphas are just plain better *than everyone else, honey. Bigger. Stronger. We're born to rule. And when we say* jump…*

The command slithered up from the ground. Despite herself, despite her *hellsheep*, Sheena's muscled tensed to jump.

…Let's just say things tend to work out in our favor.

II

FLEANCE

Parker kept talking. Each word hit Fleance like a blow.

Sheena was trying to argue. Fleance resisted the urge to move to her side. Didn't she see the tide had turned? They needed to keep Parker's attention separated so at least one of them could escape.

What about that guy? Caine? Fleance's new boss. He turned into an alpha, right? So we can—

You just don't fucking get it, do you? You can't turn into an alpha. Alphas are born, not made. Face it, sweetheart, some of us are born to rule... and some to obey.

The full reality of Parker's words sank into Fleance's bones like lead. He was right.

We always followed him, his hellhound muttered. The shame in its voice cut through him. *I thought, now that we were free, we could stop him, but he's right. We don't know anything. We didn't even know he could turn another shifter, like Sheena. What if he can take us back into his pack? We're so far away from Caine and Meaghan...*

He looked inside himself for his pack sense. It was still there, but it was faint. The other members of his pack—Caine and Meaghan, Manu and Rhys—felt more distant than the stars above.

The rapidly disappearing stars. Fleance's heart sank. Morning was coming, and given the pathways and signs, he suspected this was some sort of tourist area.

Worms slithered over his mind.

Always a fast thinker, aren't you, Flea? Parker chuckled. *You're right to be worried. Oh, not that someone will spot us. Invisibility's a handy thing that way. And we can walk through all this boiling dirt like it's nothing.* His lips stretched in a wolfish grin. *It's the tourists that concern me. If you insist on fighting like this, and something gets kicked up, or one of those pools spills over...*

He let the possibilities hang in the air.

Sheena's laughter cut through them like a knife through butter.

Sorry, I'm still hung up on alphas being 'born not made', she hooted. *Are you serious? Right to rule? I thought you Americans hated that sort of thing so much you had a war about it.*

Alphas are—

I mean, we're hanging onto the bloody Queen and it still sounds like bullshit to me!

Fleance had never heard Sheena like this before. Her psychic voice was smokey and... powerful.

And really, really sexy.

It's fate! Parker snarled, losing his cool at last. *Unchangeable!*

Unchangeable? Can you even hear yourself? You go around biting people like a bloody werewolf and you think fate can't be changed? Look at me! LOOK AT ME!

Parker jumped back as her voice darkened. The hairs on Fleance's spine stood up. That was her hellsheep talking, he realized.

Sheena didn't look at Parker. She stared past him, meeting Fleance's eyes through the coiling steam.

Neither of us were born to be hellhounds, she said. From the way he growled, Fleance knew Parker could hear her, but her words were meant for him. *If one bite can change our fate, what's to stop us changing it again? My sheep managed it.*

He was about to argue—he'd only been human, he hadn't had anything like her sheep to protect him—*I don't have anything to protect me like your sheep did,* he told her. *I wasn't a shifter. I was just... me.* His hellhound shivered as he remembered those first months. *I let you down*, it growled.

Being human doesn't make you less than being a shifter. Sheena's voice was steady. *I might just be a back-country bogan, but I know that much. I believe you *can fight back the same way my sheep did. Maybe you already did.**

Fleance tipped his head to one side, confused. *Fleance, you told me your hellhound never* wanted *to do what this dick told you. Wanting to change your fate is the first step, right? Parker might have turned you, but you choose what you do with your new life.**

I can choose? Fleance wasn't sure whether the words came from him, or his hellhound.

From the moment Fleance had been turned, Parker had steamrolled over him. He'd never even considered there was any other way. Besides, Parker was all he had. His parents were dead, his life had fallen apart, and suddenly there was this strange creature in his head...

He hadn't seen a way out. Parker had made sure of that. But now...

He raised his head. In a burst, Fleance knows that Sheena was right. Parker might have changed his fate, but it was *his* fate. He couldn't leave it between Parker's teeth.

With that realization his hellhound burned brighter than ever before. It was a clean, sharp brightness, like the morning sun reflecting off still water, not the yellow sulfur-burn he'd always known. Power pulsed through him.

He glanced at Sheena. He didn't need to say anything—understanding passed between them, quick as a flash.

Parker was still focused on Sheena. He wasn't expecting Fleance to attack. Fleance went low and fast towards his belly, teeth bared. Parker twisted away—straight into Sheena's hooves.

Crack!

The hellsheep kicked Parker in the head. He fell sideways, stunned, and before he could shake it off Fleance was at his throat.

He put one massive paw on Parker's neck. The hellsheep roared over like a steam train and put its hoof next to his paw.

Parker's eyes rolled, but his voice in Fleance's head was dripping with disdain.

This again? Face it, Flea, even if you've fooled yourself that you're as good as an alpha, you're not man enough to—aargh!

Sheena's hellsheep was too impatient to wait for him to finish. She chomped down on his neck.

The shadows that had haunted Fleance's mind since he stepped into Parker's web rearranged themselves. They blossomed with light, and weightless joy, and the sweet scent of clover.

I don't want him in your head again, she told him, her voice low and warm and only for him. *Let this be my burden to bear.*

Relief spread through his veins, honey-sweet. He never would have asked Sheena to do this, but now that she had he couldn't see it happening any other way. She knew how much it hurt him to have Parker in his head and she was too fiercely protective to put him through that again.

But the fact that she had the power to so neatly rearrange the echoes of power in his soul with a single bite...

My mate is an alpha, he thought, staring at her.

She was magnificent. Her sheep form had been adorable, but her hellsheep was ferocity on four legs. One glimpse into her burning eyes and you knew the only thing standing between you and a hellish kicking was Sheena's goodwill—which she had more of that anyone else Fleance had met.

Now, Sheena declared, leaning down to glare into Parker's eyes. *About* making *you do things...* She shrugged. *My hellsheep's still recommending I dunk you into the nearest mud pool. Honestly, right now, I think it might have a point. You're really annoying, you know that?*

Fleance had a better idea. *Remember all those shell charities, uncle? The ones that offered false hope to people after you'd got them scared they would lose everything? I think it's about time they started doing some actual work.*

Yes, his hellhound murmured. *This is right. Fixing what's wrong.*

Sheena nodded at him and he kept talking. He listed all the loose ends that had been tangling in his conscience since he was a teenager. Every family thrown out on the street, every business sunk into a pit of debt. Each one glowed like a lit fuse.

Caine just wanted you to go away, Fleance growled. *I want you to stay and make right what you did. All the world thinks you're some great philanthropist. Now you're going to actually be one. And if you get back to your old tricks…*

Sheena's laughter sizzled against his mind. By the way Parker flinched, he felt it too. *Then you'll have me to deal with,* she said.

CHAPTER 12

Sheena

Hours later…

Fleance jumped as Sheena grabbed hold of the mate bond.

"Sorry," she said, not sorry at all. "Just checking."

He made a low sound in the back of his throat and tugged her into his arms. "You're still my mate," he said. "Hellsheep."

She grinned, wide and lazy and thoroughly pleased. The mate bond sang between them, then roared as Fleance kissed her. "And you're *mine*."

They were back at the hotel. Getting there had been less of a mission than Sheena had expected. The car was munted—Sheena had explained to Fleance that that was the technical term for "has half its roof torn off"—but it still drove fine. They'd puttered back to Rotorua without incident. Sheena's blood was still blazing with adrenaline when they pulled into the hotel carpark and she hadn't been able to help taking her hellsheep's shape again to sneak back up to the room.

Being able to turn invisible had helped a lot, there. *You're doing a good job of holding back the fear,* Fleance had said as she walked half through a wall to dodge a group of hotel guests coming down the corridor. He'd shifted back to human form. Clothes intact, the bastard. *It took me months to learn that fine control. People kept running away from me and I didn't know why.*

I'm not holding anything back, Sheena had said. *I'm just... being.* She'd almost nuzzled against him, still invisible, wanting to smooth away the pain in his voice when he talked about driving people away with his unfamiliar magic. She hadn't reckoned on her hellsheep's phasing ability. She'd passed straight through Fleance, not touching him.

Which had *sucked.*

Sheena had shifted and re-solidified as soon as they were back in their room. She'd put on the dressing gown again, which was a mistake, because it was bad enough that Fleance was wearing clothes without her adding to the problem.

She slid her hands under his shirt and kissed down his neck to the thick muscle that joined to his shoulder.

Fleance buried his face in her hair. "Parker isn't going to be a problem?"

"Only if you keep talking about him while I'm trying to take your clothes off." She groaned. *Fine. He's dealt with. Back in his own hotel room at the other end of town, sulking like a wee baby. And now that I've confirmed that, I'm going to pull the blinds on him for the next while, okay?*

It was weird and more than a bit gross, being the sun around which Angus Parker's mangy psychic presence orbited, but she could block him out when she wanted. Like right now.

She pulled back to stare into Fleance's eyes. Fire kindled in them, then he blinked, and they were pure ice melt gray-blue again. All human. He reached up, his fingertips brushing her face. "Have I told you lately how incredible you are?"

"Only every ten seconds on the drive over here."

"Then I'm well below quota." Fleance's eyes were shining. She'd never seen him look this happy.

Sheena felt like she'd just woken up on Christmas morning. She couldn't stop herself pulling on the mate bond again, like a cat with a piece of string. It was bright, and pure, and wonderful, and *theirs*, untainted by anything connected to Parker. As she focused on it, it seemed to expand to fill her entire body with golden light.

Fleance's fingers tensed against her cheek, then gentled as the electricity thrumming through her skin met the same energy humming in his. *You're incredible.*

"And you're mine."

Fleance laughed and kissed her. The mate bond sang, a single pure note that thrummed through Sheena's whole body.

I think I need to stop saying I've figured out how being a shifter works, he said, his voice curling against her mind like a happy cat. *A happy hellhound*, she corrected herself. *Alphas, being turned into a hellhound… The world keeps proving me wrong.*

That goes for both of us. Sheena nuzzled against him. *I thought I had to go far away from my family to find out who I really was. Instead, protecting them showed me that I didn't need to pretend to be strong. I already was.* She paused. *Well, except for the whole snorting fire thing.*

I think your sheep always was a hellsheep at heart.

And you must have been a hellhound.

Fleance froze. Sheena stopped kissing him but kept her arms around his shoulders so he knew she wasn't going anywhere. *Not the way your dick uncle does it. Which clearly isn't working for him; the guy looks like a stiff wind would knock him to pieces. I mean... you're a good person. You want to protect people. And that's what your hellhound wanted to do, too.*

It didn't do a good job of it. Fleance's face went still, then he caught Sheena's eye and let his mouth twist bitterly. *Hurting people isn't justice.*

"It's been through a lot. You've been through a lot. And now you've got me." She smiled and bit him gently on the chin. "If your hellhound gets confused again, I'll be here to sort you out."

He let out a short breath. Almost a laugh. "My alpha."

Sheena *did* laugh. "I thought we agreed that alphas were bullshit?"

"Being born an alpha, maybe." Fleance ran one finger along her jawline. "Sheena, you're my mate. But any shifter who looks at you will know you're more than that."

She stared at him. "You're biased."

"Obviously." He tipped his head back, regarding her with so much longing her knees went weak. "I'd be a fool if I wasn't biased. And I'd be a fool if I couldn't see that you should be the center of my universe as well as of my heart."

Sheena shook her head. Her? An alpha? Sheep didn't have alphas. Sure, she'd... sort of taken over Angus Parker's mind, but...

Am I an alpha? she asked her hellsheep.

I AM, it said at once, then got back to napping. *You're no use*, she grumbled at it, and said to Fleance:

"But you *have* an alpha. Back in Pine Valley."

"No." The lines at the edges of his mouth deepened. "Being near Parker again did something to my pack sense. I don't think I have an alpha anymore. Or a pack. And that's... bad."

Sheena looked harder at him and gasped. His eyes were burning hellhound-bright, but deep in their centers was a hint of the same dark rot that Parker's eyes had held.

Was that why Parker's hellhound looked so sick? He didn't have a pack. Caine had taken every hellhound Parker had ever turned and cast him loose alone. Maybe hellhounds were pack animals for a reason. Maybe they *needed* that connection. It would explain why Fleance and the others hadn't been able to break free. Their hellhounds knew they needed a pack to survive, and since none of them knew about the alpha trick—whatever the alpha trick Sheena's hellsheep had pulled actually was—they'd stayed. Some instinct must have told them that any pack, even Parker's, was better than none.

She sent her question down the mate bond and felt his response almost at once. He was weary, and hopeful... and she was right.

"Okay," she said, scrambling for ideas. "We'll go find Parker again, this time I'll let you chomp down on him and you can go alpha and—"

"No." Fleance's jaw worked. "I'm not going to hurt people anymore and that includes not using my asshole uncle as a punching bag. Besides, that wouldn't fix things."

"You wouldn't be alone anymore. You'd be an alpha with a, a very small, very dickhead-heavy pack, but it would stop... whatever this is."

"But it would leave you packless." Parker winced and jerked his head to the side. "And whatever this is, I won't let it happen to you."

"Then you need to go back to the States, right? Back to your alpha, Caine. We can sort that. I already have a ticket—not that we need to go on the same flight, well, flights, but..."

"No." He took her hands in his and kissed them gently. "I don't want to go back to the Guinnesses. Caine is fine, he's nothing like Parker, but I still didn't have any choice about joining his pack. There is another option, though. I..."

His voice stopped in his throat. He was staring at their joined hands, not meeting her eyes. She uncurled one finger and tipped his head up so he was looking at her.

"What can I do?" she asked.

Fleance's eyes were dark—with longing, with exhaustion, with that cold, wretched loneliness of the hound without a pack. "Claim me." He swallowed. "Like you did Parker."

"No." She put a finger on Fleance's lips before he could reply. Her heart was racing. "That's not a *no* no. I would do anything to help you. I will claim you, but not like with him."

Relief washed over her, full of the light of the mate bond, and Fleance pressed his forehead against her hands. "Thank you," he whispered.

A shiver went down her spine. Half freaked out, half... excited?

Fleance was already hers. They were bound together by the mate bond, as equals. If she wanted to claim Fleance—and oh, hell, did she—did that make her a bad person? Like Parker?

She peered at the solar system whirling inside her head. Her in the middle and the single soul circling like a planet around the sun—Angus Parker.

No, she decided. She wouldn't be like Parker. She *wasn't* like Parker. Fleance wanted her to claim him and her wanting the same thing wasn't about controlling him. He was trusting her to be even more intimately connected to him than the mate bond allowed.

In a way it would make her as vulnerable to him as he was to her.

Maybe that's why Parker ruled with his boot on his pack's necks, Sheena thought, and immediately pushed the thought away. She didn't give a shit about Parker right now. The most important person in her life was right in front of her.

She rested one hand on Fleance's chest and kissed him.

"I'm going to clean my teeth first," she told him.

Two minutes later:

"This is torture," Fleance groaned from where he was sitting on the edge of the tub.

I'm not going to claim you with dirty teeth! Sheena told him. Again. **I bit Parker with these teeth! Well, with my hellsheep's version of these teeth. Either way, that's fucking feral.**

"Fine." Fleance stood up. "Then I'm going to take a shower."

This is torture, she thought, watching him in the mirror.

Fleance stripped off his jacket and dropped it on the floor. He was bare-chested underneath. Sheena had borrowed his shirt for the drive back into town, and promptly disintegrated it when she shifted to sneak through the corridors. Fleance's skin was scuffed with dirt, as though he'd brought along the mud he'd picked up in his hellhound form the same way he shifted with his clothes intact.

His pants joined his jacket on the floor. Then his boxers. Sheena let out a toothpaste-flavored groan as he stepped into the tub. His body was pure muscular power, honed and polished until his every movement was like a dance. A sexy shower dance. He stood under the water, turning so that it ran over every inch of his body. Over his face, his toned chest, the hard lines of his abs. It trickled down his hips, caught in the deep grooves of his V and then…

Sheena groaned out loud and threw her toothbrush down. Fleance crossed his arms and leaned against the shower wall.

"You've already had a shower," he protested as she slid her dressing gown over her shoulders.

"Hush," she commanded as she stepped into the shower with him. Hot water pounded down on her shoulders, but she barely noticed it. All her attention was on her mate.

It wasn't just dirt darkening his skin. There were bruises, too. She touched her fingertips to a livid mark on his ribs. "When did this happen?"

"During the fight. You were there, remember?"

She remembered Fleance limping in his hellhound form and protectiveness rose up inside her, hot and fierce. "You're hurt—"

"But you're not. That's what is important."

"No, it's not." She soaped up a cloth and ran it gently over the bruise. Then over his chest, his arms, every part of him that she could reach. There were more bruises hidden under the dirt, and scratches. Most of them were already scabbing over but enough were still unhealed enough to stain the water red as it whirled into the drain.

Sheena looked into his eyes. "If we're ever in a fight like that again, you have to let me take some hits. I won't let you put yourself on the front line again." She pulled him down for a kiss. *Not without me by your side.*

If we're in a fight again, he agreed. *My job is to make sure that doesn't happen. As your mate and as your pack.*

Good luck. I don't think my hellsheep has the same opinion on fighting as you. Or me, for that matter.

Fleance smiled against her lips. *I'm still a hellhound. If your hellsheep needs to be herded…*

You wouldn't dare.

He stroked her sides, drawing her closer. *You're not my alpha yet.*

She leaned towards the heat that emanated from his entire body. She was hot, too, her body straining for his touch. Every brush of his hands on her skin, his lips against hers, made her burn more fiercely. Desire was a weight strung between them, pulling them both in.

But she didn't want to rush. The last time had felt almost brutal with desperation. There'd been no space for her to cherish his body. This *man*, who was already so much a part of her and yet about whom she still had so much to learn.

She let her hands drift down from his chest, trailing a river of droplets over his stomach. The darkness was still in his eyes, but despite his bruises, he wasn't badly hurt.

Is it okay if we take this slowly?

His eyes burned. *Of course.*

There was no desperation now, just a deep hunger and longing and the promise of a future stretching out far ahead. Sheena pushed Fleance into the corner and pulled his head down to kiss him while her other hand explored the hard line of his collarbone. She trailed her fingertips along his shoulder muscles, amazed all over again that every inch of this gorgeous man was *hers.*

Fleance moaned as her hand drifted lower. His thighs tensed at her touch, and when he grabbed her and lifted her with her back against the wall the only reason it wasn't a surprise was because she'd felt the mate bond thrum with intention a split second before. Sheena laughed and kicked her legs half-heartedly.

"Hey. Who's claiming who, here?"

Fleance kissed her, which wasn't a reply. She dug her fingertips into the tight muscles at the base of his neck and he groaned and rested his head on her shoulder, still holding her up against the wall.

I'm yours, he murmured, his voice a prayer in her head.

She lay a row of kisses down the side of his neck, following the thick band of muscle that was still too tight, too tense. *Only if I'm yours, too,* she breathed back, nibbling gently. He moaned at the scrape of her teeth.

Yes.

Sheena's whole body thrilled. The mate bond lit her from the inside, held her in orbit with Fleance, but this was a different, darker excitement. The mate bond was fate. This was something new. Something they were both choosing with all their hearts.

She wrapped her legs more tightly around him. The line of his cock jutted against her inner thigh. Her skin was wet, slick from the water still pouring over Fleance's back and shoulders, but she burned wherever Fleance touched her.

He dragged her head up and kissed her again, deep and slow with a moan that rumbled through his lips directly to her core. She wriggled impatiently, realigning herself against the glorious hardness of his cock.

He murmured wordlessly against her lips and bucked his hips. The head of his cock pressed into her, hot and thick and so good her whole body curled with exquisite thrill. If Fleance hadn't been holding her up she would have slithered deliciously to the floor. With his arms around her, she let herself revel in every second of sensation as he pushed inch by inch into her. Her soul had been reshaped over the last day, twisted into a new form and then taking a new shape for itself, but her human body remembered this feeling; remembered the press of Fleance's fingertips in her skin as he thrust hilt-deep into her, the soft gasp that arrived in her heart along the mate bond a millisecond before it reached her ears. The wonder in every stroke of his hands across her body. The doubled, tripled rush of feeling, skin to skin, heart to heart, the mate bond amplifying every touch and every touch making the light inside her burn brighter. Not inevitable. Hard-won, and precious, and *hers*.

She let out an involuntary gasp as he drove into her. Every inch of her body, inside and out, hummed with a building, electric arousal. Fleance kissed her and she bit down on his lip. Not hard enough to draw blood; the roar of desire that spilled out of him was so intense she gasped and released him.

Then she kissed him even harder than before, twisting his hair around her fingers and grinding into him. Her nipples grazed his chest and she cried out as he slid one hand up to cup her breast, a hungry moan on his breath.

"Please," he groaned, and inside her head: *Please.*

He moved one hand to the back of her head and guided it down to his neck. *This is more Dracula than I was thinking,* she murmured, and his answering bittersweet chuckle whirled inside her like a spring breeze.

Her hellsheep reared up inside her. When she bit down on the fine lines that were all that remained of his turning scars, fire filled her veins. The constellation in her head flared; a new satellite appeared in orbit around her sun.

She dug her fingertips into Fleance's scalp, her breaths coming fast and hot. *Now you.*

His teeth grazed her shoulder. Heat pooled beneath her skin, a surge of magma simmering beneath the surface and spiked with lightning. She didn't know whether she was kissing him with her lips or her teeth as the pleasure that had been building inside her since she first followed him into the shower exploded. She cried out; her body went tight as a bowstring then released, not once but over and over.

Fleance clutched her to him; he buried his face in her hair, holding her as her body rocked with pleasure. "Oh, God, Sheena," he gasped. The heavens whirled inside her head. The light from her heart flooded the skies.

Then he was carrying her out of the bathroom, throwing her down onto the bed and bearing down on her. His need spiked through the mate bond, a wordless question that burned in her veins. He'd come so close to losing her and it had left a coldness in the center of his heart that only taking her completely would warm again. Hard, and fast, and his.

She nodded and he thrust into her in one smooth movement, fucking her into the mattress so hard that she forgot how to breathe. Their breaths mingled, short and sharp, gasps no longer than heartbeats and her heart beating so hard it filled her head. She'd never felt so alive. So completely present within her own body.

Fleance kissed her again. She wrapped her arms and legs around him and kissed him back. Then his lips were on her neck, teeth scraping against her skin and the universe spinning inside her head. She dragged his head back up, her fingers tangling in his hair, and nipped the tender skin beneath his ear.

He groaned low in his throat and grabbed her hips, angling them so that his next thrust went so deep Sheena saw stars. She bit him harder than she'd meant to, and then his teeth were in her shoulder, his fingers digging into her hips and arse, and she was driving herself up against him as hard as he was thrusting her into the bed. Something cracked a few feet above her head. The whole bed jolted down. Fleance didn't react. He gathered her to him, his body hot and hard against hers. With one final thrust he bottomed out inside her, filling her completely. He buried his face in her hair with a groan that reverberated to her very core. Sheena's body responded, caught like a fish on a line as his cock flexed inside her. Pleasure twisted white-hot and sharp inside her and came apart with a crash as his orgasm pushed her past the brink again.

Mine, she thought as he collapsed on top of her, his chest heaving. She curled against him, feeling totally, decadently pleased with herself. He raised his head to stare at her and his eyes were hazy with pleasure.

There was something more than the mate bond between them, now. Something that hummed unsaid on the edge of every breath, and in the pale flames that flickered in his eyes.

She pushed herself up and bit down on his lower lip, just to be sure.

There.

When she'd bitten Parker, the change to her mental landscape had been immediate and clear.

He was a greasy black mark at the corner of her mind, but firmly under *her* control. But this, with Fleance…

She looked down at herself, at the red marks where he'd dragged his teeth along her skin, then glanced back up at him with one eyebrow raised.

Fleance reddened.

"I guess that worked, then," Sheena whispered. She could feel her own face glowing, as though putting words to the impossible wonder growing inside her was crossing some sort of boundary. She stretched one hand up to where Fleance was bracing himself above her and twined her fingers between his. "Now no one's going to take you from me."

"And no one will take you from me." He kissed her and Sheena closed her eyes, letting her mind fall into the new constellation that had formed in her soul: two stars, dancing around each other, the center of each other's universes.

12

FLEANCE

Someone was knocking on the door.

Fleance's hellhound was alert at once. Fleance's human side followed—groggily—and, curled against his chest, Sheena gave a groan that sounded like it came from the depths of her soul.

He cocked his head on one side and listened. Knocking *and* shouting, he decided; and it wasn't him they were after.

"Sheena," he murmured. *We've got company.*

She stuck her hand in his mouth and prodded his jaw so that he bit down on it. "You're the alpha now. You deal with it."

"I don't think it works that way," he whispered as his hellhound quirked its head, considering her suggestion. He wasn't surprised when it tucked its nose under its paws. It was as happy as he was to let Sheena take charge, so long as while she did the roaring in headfirst, he was at her side to protect her.

He nudged her again. "Or maybe because you're the alpha, you could send me to do your bidding…"

She sat bolt upright and swore. He opened his mouth to say he'd been joking, but she was already off the bed and scouring the floor for something to wear.

"I know you were joking," she said, holding one hand palm-up to interrupt him before he'd even managed to get a word out. "It's not you, it's—oh God. I'm so sorry for what's about to happen. This is all my fault…"

The part of the mattress she'd been lying on already felt cold without her, but Fleance had more to worry about than the empty space at his side. He sat up. Whoever was pounding on the door was pounding on his brain, too. Shifters, sending out an open telepathic broadcast to anyone in range.

Two voices, he thought, but he couldn't make out what they were saying. They were overlapping too much.

"Do you know who that is?" he asked Sheena.

"Yes!" she cried. "Where's my bloody—anything? Dressing gown?"

"In the bathroom."

Sheena swore. She made it halfway across the room before the door burst open.

Two women fought to each get through at the same time. One had the same round face and sturdy figure as Sheena; the other had darker skin and was whip-thin, with tattoos snaking up her arms.

Both wore expressions of relief as they caught sight of Sheena. Her own expression was far less good natured as she grabbed a cushion from the sofa to cover herself.

Fleance sniffed the air, and: *Sheep*, his hellhound thought, focusing on the first one. *And… some sort of bird.*

"Oh, sweetie, you're safe—" the sheep shifter began, as the other woman burst out: "We've been worried sick! Your mum's been blowing up Fi's phone—"

"*GO AWAY!*" Sheena shrieked at them both.

"Oh, come off your high horse, it's nothing we haven't seen before," the first woman tutted, gesturing at Sheena as she tried to cover herself.

"Ah…" The bird shifter plucked at her arm and she turned to the bed.

Fleance waved weakly.

The sheep shifter's eyebrows shot up. "Now *there's* something I haven't seen before."

"OUT!" Sheena jumped on the bed, straddling Fleance, and threw a pillow at the women with point-blank accuracy. Fleance struggled out of the blankets and started to wrap one around his mate as she screamed at the women he was beginning to suspect were her aunts.

"I'LL TELL YOU!" she yelled, in response—he guessed—to a telepathic question he hadn't been privy to. "JUST LET ME SHOWER FIRST! CLOTHES!"

She kept shouting until the door closed behind them both, then collapsed onto the bed. Fleance made sure she fell into his arms before they both hit the mattress.

Sheena pressed against him, grumbling wordlessly. He kissed the top of her head.

"Those were your aunts?"

Sheena sighed. "In their defense, I did completely forget to check in with them. In my defense..." She banged her forehead against his chest. "Oh, God. Can I just stay here forever? I mean, they at least know I'm alive now. So really there's no need for me to ever see them again."

"I wouldn't argue. But what are the chances of your aunts busting that door down if you don't make an appearance?"

She raised her head and groaned. "Too high." Sheena stretched, but didn't make any move to leave the bed—or Fleance's arms. Her body was warm and soft against his.

"Shame." He closed his eyes, luxuriating in his pack sense. Letting himself sink into it like this, no hesitation, no fear, was an entirely new sensation. Even with Caine, he'd been wary, but now, Sheena was his sun. He basked in her light.

The shorter one is my Aunt Fiona, Sheena explained. *She's a Valais Blacknose shifter, a sheep like me. Rena is her mate, she's a tūī shifter. That's a sort of native bird. God, this is just so bloody typical of my family.*

Does your family always come running to the rescue when you get into trouble?

No chance! I'm barely allowed to sniff at trouble back home. She sighed and then winced. "Oh, God. I never called. The last thing my aunts heard from me was me screaming and dropping my bloody cellphone when Parker came at me."

"No wonder they came out in force. Your family must—"

He stopped. Sheena was making a noise that was half-terror, half-frustration.

"My family. My—" She stopped and squeezed her eyes shut, mouthing numbers.

Fleance raised one eyebrow. "Counting sheep?" he guessed.

She groaned again. "My *whole* family. We'd better start moving before they all get up here."

Her *whole family.* Fleance had expected a handful of people. Parents, the two aunts, maybe a grandparent or two.

He stared at the congregation crowded into the hotel foyer with something approaching horror.

Sheena's voice pressed against his mind as she grabbed his arm. *That's Fiona and Rena, you know them already. Fiona's parents are the ones who look like they came straight off the farm. And my aunt and uncle Tara and Mack and their kids my cousins Matiu and Wiremu and... um, a lot of other cousins whose names I really should know... Uh... Mum! Dad!*

She hurried forwards, and Fleance lengthened his stride so he wasn't left being dragged behind. She stopped in front of a couple who immediately pulled her into a spine-crushing embrace.

"Love, we were so worried!"

"Fiona and Rena told us everything, we came as fast as we could."

"Are you hurt? I *knew* we shouldn't have let you take the bus by yourself—"

Sheena reared back as her mother tried to wipe her face with a handkerchief. "*Mum!*"

There was a brief buzz of private telepathic speech, and both of Sheena's parents turned their attention to Fleance. Not just her parents. He felt like he was being backed into a corner by a very large, very short mob.

Sheena drew herself up. Her cheeks burned with pride. "Mum, Dad, this is Fleance. Fleance, these are my parents, Heather and Mike."

"Pleasure," Fleance said, shaking their hands.

Fleance is my mate, Sheena blurted out, her telepathic voice ringing with mingled embarrassment and pride.

You don't need to tell us that, chook, her father told her. He clasped Fleance's shoulder. *I'm guessing you're the one we have to thank for getting our Sheena out of whatever was happening here alive?*

Fleance looked down at his mate. Her love for her family was clear—as was her strangled huff of frustration as her dad suggested she hadn't had anything to do with defeating Parker. She caught his eye and the mate bond twanged with—hope? A warning?

"Actually," Fleance said, wrapping one arm around her, "Sheena's the one who saved me."

It was definitely a warning, he decided as his mind was swamped by a dozen shifters wanting to know the whole story.

Sheena gave him a wry look. *You would have been better off taking all the credit,* she said, slipping her arm through his.

He wasn't sure who made the decision to drive en masse back to Silver Springs. He suspected it was Sheena's mother, in some sheepish, non-alpha form of complete and utter control. The hotel staff were relieved to see them go, although they kept their relief professionally hidden. One midnight fire alarm—which Fleance had no doubt would appear on his room bill—was bad enough without adding an entire sheep shifter clan to the situation.

It was a clear afternoon—no, Fleance realized, it was morning again. How long had he and Sheena been asleep?

The flock drove in a single mob down the motorway to the Silver Springs turnoff, and jostled down the winding, decorative drive through the houses.

Or what was left of them.

Sheena's dad hissed a breath in through his teeth. "What's the story here, then?"

Heather clicked her tongue. "Weren't you listening before? Poor Fiona, all the work she's put in."

"Was that what you were trying to dig out of her? I thought you were bothering her about Christmas again."

"Well she's hardly going to be able to host it now, is she? With the whole place gone up in flames."

Squashed into the back seat, Fleance caught Sheena's eye. Somehow in the crush to get everyone into various cars, Sheena had ended up wrapped in a blanket and clutching a thermos. She grimaced, tucked the thermos down the side of the seat, and took his hand.

Just say the word, and we can phase out of here and go bush. Her psychic voice had a hint of smoke in it. Not sulfur—woodsmoke.

He smiled. *I don't mind.*

Sheena rolled her eyes and wriggled against him. *Did you consider that I might mind?*

Shame. He grinned and dropped a kiss on top of her head. *I'm glad to meet your family. You've seen where I came from—* He tried not to wince. *—now I get to meet the people who helped you turn out so wonderful.*

I feel like I should resent the suggestion that I'm not responsible for my own wonderful-ness. Sheena wrinkled her nose. *Except I'm pretty sure that's my hellsheep talking.*

Her eyes slid past him to the wreckage outside, and fire shimmered at the edges of her irises. The texture of her parents' conversation in the front of the car didn't change; neither of them had noticed anything.

We're definitely going to have to do something about that, Sheena murmured as the ruined houses passed by outside, and her psychic voice tasted like a bonfire.

The mob reformed outside the only house that had been left unscathed by Parker's attack: her aunts' patchwork villa. Fiona and Rena were standing together at the front door. Fleance watched them exchange an exhausted glance.

Heather tutted. "They could have left us a better park!" she complained, hauling the steering wheel around and blocking another car in as she found a spot.

Sheena squeezed Fleance's hand and slithered into the tiny gap between their car and the next. *You can't say I didn't warn you.*

Fleance frowned as he opened his door. *What do you mean?*

He soon found out.

Relatives surrounded him in a swarm. All of them were shouting. Hands clapped him on the shoulder, none of them clearly connected to any of the people moving around him. Names went in one ear and out the other. Someone pressed a filled roll into Fleance's hand.

"Better get stuck in now, mate, they're a pack of magpies around here!" someone—possibly the same someone, possibly not—bawled in the vicinity of his eardrum.

"Thanks," he said, feeling dizzy. When had he made it all the way up to the house? His brain hadn't been involved in any decision to move, that was for sure. The flock had moved, and he'd been swept along with it.

He was beginning to understand what Sheena meant about going along with the flock. And why her sheep sometimes wanted to run in its own direction.

"No worries. Someone's gotta remember to keep everyone fed while Heather's on the warpath."

He had no idea who the man was who'd just given him a sandwich. *A cousin,* Sheena said when he sent her a desperate question. He couldn't see her and was seriously considering resorting to tracing her using his pack sense, when she pushed through the crowd. He grabbed her hand, trying not to feel like he was grabbing for a lifesaver.

How many cousins do you have?

Jeez, I don't know. Too many?

Fleance barely managed to take a single bite of the filled roll before he found himself dragged into the kitchen and installed at a rough-hewn dining table. Someone pressed a bottle of beer into his free hand as Sheena elbowed her way in beside him. The two of them were at the heart of a whirling storm of her family, all emanating concern and curiosity.

"I'm *fine*," Sheena said in response to a question he didn't catch. "Really! Better than fine. I'm not going to catch cold from being outside for half a minute."

You could just shift and show them, Fleance suggested. She shot him a dirty look.

Sure, if we want half of them shifting in shock and trampling through the house. Sheena snorted.

Her mother narrowed her eyes. It was a distressingly familiar expression, and Fleance wondered if Sheena knew just how much of her own stubborn nature was part of her sheep shifter heritage, not something new from her hellsheep's influence.

Someone held a phone up, screen towards Fleance and Sheena. A young woman who looked Sheena's age, with long dark hair and what was now a familiar expression of mixed exasperation and worry on her face, stared out at them.

"Aroha!" Sheena cried out.

"I can't *believe* you!" the woman on the phone yelled back, her voice tinny through the speakers. "I stop talking to you for half a day and you burn down an entire village!"

"That wasn't me! It was a *hellhound*!"

"A *what?!*"

Her mother, Heather, cleared her throat. On-screen, Aroha slammed her hands against her face and groaned. "That's enough," Heather said placidly. She turned to the two of them sitting on the picnic bench. "Let's deal with the important things first."

Fleance saw Sheena revving herself up to complain again that she wasn't hurt, she wasn't too cold or too tired or too hungry she was *fine*, when Heather followed up with: "How did you two meet?"

The mate bond trembled with indignation, but Sheena covered it well. Fleance hid his grin. *Now you're indignant she's not asking after you?*

Hush, you. Sheena ran her fingers through her hair. "Funny you should say that. I was about to run into a burning building—"

"*Sheena!*"

"—but then Fleance turned up and ran in for me, which was real helpful. It meant that I had the first bash at this dickhead hellhound shifter who turned up…"

"No!"

Fleance began to suspect as the story unraveled that despite her protestations Sheena actually quite liked scandalizing her family. He joined in the retelling where necessary, but mostly sat and enjoyed Sheena winding up her audience. Even in Pine Valley, he'd never been so close to the center of such a clearly loving group of people.

These people were *real* family. Not just the shared blood he had with Angus. Even if Sheena couldn't remember all of her cousins' names or how they were related to her—and he gathered, from a few whispered remarks, that she wasn't alone in that—they were all ride or die for her. People talked about herd mentality like it was a bad thing, but if it meant everyone coming together to protect one member of the herd from an outside threat?

He wrapped his hand around Sheena's as she skipped over the non-PG parts of the story and began to describe their early-morning car race out of town. The mate bond hummed, and he let some of his feelings filter through it: his joy at seeing her surrounded by her family, how new it was for him to see people all coming together like this.

How it felt like a perfect Christmas miracle.

She raised one eyebrow but didn't say anything to him until she reached a dramatic pause in her story: "There was nothing I could do. If Fleance didn't agree to obey Parker's every order, I'd be under his control forever."

Everyone gasped. Sheena's aunt Rena, who was standing by the door, covered her face. "This is all my fault," she muttered. "If we hadn't let him get his claws into us…"

Fiona put an arm around her shoulders and held her close.

Sheena's eyes sparkled mischievously. "But then, just when it looked like there was no way out—"

"You must have been *terrified*," another aunt/cousin/miscellaneous relation burst out.

"Well, yeah, I—"

"But you shouldn't feel bad about not being able to get away," another relative said quickly. "We all know—"

"Poor wee lamb!" Another aunt—*How many does she have?*—squeezed Sheena's hand. "You must have been so frightened!"

Sheena's cheeks started to turn red. The smell of burning lanolin filled the air. Fleance cleared his throat. *Babe...*

She gave him a long-suffering look. *See? They literally can't imagine any scenario in which I did more than get in the way.*

"And out by the geysers! We all know what you're like with the thermal wonderland around here."

"Ooh, yes. Remember last time they came to visit? That sinkhole?"

Sheena's cheeks were the color of traffic lights. "I—"

"But you *did* get away." Her mother, Heather, turned kind eyes on Fleance. "We're so glad you were there, Fleance. I don't want to think what might have happened if you weren't around."

She still thinks I saved Sheena? Even after what I said back at the hotel? No wonder his mate was glowing with frustration. Her family were all loving and supportive... and couldn't even conceive that she might have been the one who'd saved him. Who'd saved them *both*.

"I hardly had anything to do with it," he tried to say, but no one was listening. He glanced over at Sheena. He wasn't stupid enough to send calming thoughts through the mate bond to his beloved but was relieved when he saw that despite the conversation battering back and forth over their heads, she looked more amused than enraged.

I'm not mad, she explained, shrugging. *I just... this is exactly what I expected. Total support, and total treating me like a particularly dim soft toy.*

"Where is this Parker now, then?" her father asked.

"Someone must have dealt with him."

"I bet it's one of those dragons she was talking about. Far, a dragon shifter! I hope we get to meet them."

"Oh—look at her, she's all red. She must be feeling sick, poor thing."

"Good thing that dragon showed up."

"She does look feverish, doesn't she? Sheena, lamb, do you want a Panadol? I've got some in my purse."

"I'm not sick!" Sheena burst out and slammed her hands palm-down on the table. "And there wasn't a—"

Of course she's sick. This is just classic Sheena. Come on, I'll put the jug on for a lemon and honey drink.

"I don't need a lemon and honey! Seriously, Mum, I'm not a kid anymore!" Something inside Sheena must have snapped. Even her acceptance of her family's view of her couldn't survive everything. "I'll show you—"

The room quietened.

"You'll always be my little lamb, sweetheart," her mother told her. "And you're not the only one who's had a long day." She rubbed her eyes, suddenly looking exhausted, and Fleance felt Sheena's heart lurch. He reached out to her gently and she leaned into his touch.

"Oh," Sheena mumbled. She whispered into Fleance's mind: *I thought it was normal that my whole family would somehow show up out of nowhere, but it's not, is it? They all raced here from across the whole bloody country because they thought I'd got myself into real trouble this time.* Sheena bit her lip. *Gotta admit, I was planning on going for the whole 'surprise, motherfuckers', but now, I think...*

She stretched one hand across the table and took her mother's hand. "I'm all right, Mum. Really. You don't need to worry about me anymore."

"Of course I need to worry about you!" Heather sniffed, half-laughing. "My little lamb, always getting in over her head."

Sheena laughed. "It'll take a bit more to get in over my head these days, Mum." She squeezed Heather's hand. "When Parker bit me and my body tried to fight off the hellhound infection, my sheep... disappeared."

"But it came back," her mother interjected. She closed her eyes briefly and Fleance felt a strange pressure through the mate bond; the feeling of being watched, but experienced through someone else's skin. "I can still see you there, part of our big old flock."

"It did come back. Just… a bit different."

"What do you mean?"

Sheena's smile started off nervous, but she clearly couldn't hold it back for long. Glee spread across her face, bright and shining, and Fleance wondered how much of the energy burning behind her eyes was her inner animal and how much was herself, thrilling with excitement. "I didn't turn into a hellhound. But I didn't totally *not* turn into one, either. And you don't have to worry about me now, because I'm not a little lamb anymore. I'm…"

Sparks flashed over her skin. Her body shimmered at the edges, light and shadows dancing like sunspots, and the smell of wool and woodsmoke filled the air.

…a hellsheep. Sheena's voice crackled like a bonfire.

Fleance blinked as the lights of Sheena's shift temporarily dazzled him. When his vision cleared, Sheena's hellsheep was taking up more space in the small kitchen than he'd thought existed. Fire sprouted from its eyes and licked along its curly black-and-white coat.

It got exactly the reaction that Fleance suspected Sheena had been hoping for—*before* she'd decided to ease her family into the news rather than jump it on them. He wondered just how much her hellsheep was steamrolling Sheena's gentler feelings. Not that it wanted to scare anyone—he could feel as clear as his own thoughts that it was just overjoyed to be able to show off.

Her mother stood up, mouth wide open. Several possibly-aunts swore; one could-be-an-uncle made a sound that was close to a shriek. There was a flutter of wings by the door, and suddenly a small bird with darkly iridescent plumage and a white bit of fluff at its throat was perched in Fiona's hair. She patted it absently, mouthing something Fleance couldn't make out.

See? Not so little,* Sheena said, kicking her back legs happily. She'd half-phased through the window, Fleance realized belatedly; that was how she could still 'fit' in there without crowding everyone else out. **I'll have to try a lot harder to get in over my head now!**

Her mother just stared at her. Beside her, Sheena's dad pushed his hat back off his head.

"I'll be damned," he muttered.

And as for Parker… Sheena looked over her parents' heads—which wasn't difficult—towards

Fiona and the bird-shaped Rena. *He's not in charge anymore. I am. I'm the alpha of his pack. And I'm going to make sure he fixes everything he broke here. Down to the last singed flax bush.*

Heather was still staring at her. "Sheena, you're…"

Sheena lowered her massive head to look at her. A hint of clover mingled with her hellfire scent. *Finally big enough to deal with the trouble I keep running into by myself?*

Heather let out a breath that was half-sigh, half-laughter. She drew herself up. "Big enough? Look at you! Do you know how much extra energy a form like that must need? And you haven't eaten a thing since you got here!" She put her hands on her hips and shouted over Sheena's huge, slightly-on-fire shoulder to a group of men gathered around a grill outside. "Kev! Gav! Hurry up with those sausages!" She reached up and patted the side of Sheena's nose with a smile on her face. "I don't care how big you are, my wee lamb. I'll still worry about you as long as I know you're out there getting into mischief. That's my job."

"She's got me to help her with that, now," Fleance added. Heather turned her eyes to him.

"If that's meant to reassure me," she said, a sparkle in her eye, "then you have a lot to learn about my Sheena. You'll end up helping her into trouble more than you help her out of it."

"That sounds just fine to me," Fleance said, and the golden rope that connected him to Sheena glowed as brightly as the twin suns in the center of his mind.

Much later, after Heather had made good on her threat to feed Sheena until she was bursting in order to fuel her hellsheep properly, the two of them managed to slip away into the trees.

Sheena had managed to pull her clothes with her when she shifted back into human form. She squeezed herself up against him, sliding one hand up under his jacket. A thrill shivered across his skin at her touch.

That could have gone worse, she said. *I think they like you.*

Fleance stretched his hearing out to catch the conversation from one of the nearer clusters. *I think they're already picking out baby names.*

Oh, God. If we don't act quickly we'll wake up tomorrow morning with the rest of our lives planned out for us. Sheena nuzzled against him with a groan.

"You're lucky to have a family that cares about you." Fleance put his arms around her.

"And you're brave, saying that out loud where they might hear you," she quipped, then sighed. "I hate to admit it, but you might be right. I've always thought they smothered me, but seeing them all here today… it's because they care about me. Not just because they want to wrap me up in cotton wool." She snorted, and a puff of amusement raced along the mate bond. "In retrospect, if they'd *actually* been smothering me properly all these years, I wouldn't have caused them nearly as much stress as I have done."

"Really, they're the victims here."

"You are so right. Better say it a bit louder, the aunties will love you forever." She pulled his head down and snuck a kiss that drove the last of the strain of the previous few days from his shoulders. "What about your family? Not Parker. Your pack back in Pine Valley."

"They're not my pack anymore, remember?" he reminded her with a fond grimace. "You took care of that."

They walked deeper into the trees together, picking their way over frozen leaf litter and tough, winding roots. The tree ferns and palm-like plants looked more exotic the longer Fleance looked at them, and he couldn't help but wonder aloud what they would look like in the summer.

"Very green," Sheena said flatly. "These ones have white flowers, but for the most part it's just green, green, green. And—my bag!"

She dashed over to a bright blue backpack, which was lying abandoned at the base of one of the fern-like trees.

"I dropped it when I smelled the smoke..." She trailed off, frowning. "That feels like years ago, now."

"You were planning a trip, weren't you?"

"Huh! I was meant to fly out of here tomorrow evening. Still am, technically. Auckland to Honolulu to San Francisco, and then... wherever the road took me. Meaning wherever I ended up after my sheep does its thing." She stared at her pack and nibbled on her lower lip. "You know, before I met you, I thought that once I found my mate everything would slot into place. I'd put down roots wherever I was and get stuck into the rest of my life. Which would mean right here, I guess."

Right here? Fleance let the thought sink in. Then he looked up again, at the frozen forest that surrounded them, and let that sink in, too.

He'd barely had time to appreciate New Zealand as a place. His arrival and memory of everything from Auckland south was a blur, and if he'd thought about Rotorua at all, he'd thought it was a fittingly hellish backdrop to his mission. The sulfuric gases, boiling mud pits and steam gushing from natural vents at the sides of the roads had seemed eerily apt.

Now, though, he could see the beauty in it. This landscape was strange, almost alien, like the photos he'd seen of Yellowstone, but made stranger still by the unfamiliar trees and bushes and the birdsong that fluted from hidden branches. The landscape seemed new and somehow incredibly ancient at the same time, and somehow alive. It wasn't monstrous, or some vision of hell. It was beautiful.

"I could see myself staying," he said, pressing his lips against the top of Sheena's head.

She stilled, then looked up at him. "What? Nah."

"But you just said—"

"And what about your family? I know—" She waved away his objections. "—I know they're not your *pack* anymore, but family doesn't have to mean who's related to you by blood, or by whatever we're calling this hellhound stuff. Magic shit. It's the people who are important to you. And you wouldn't have come all this way to stop Parker from hurting everyone you left behind if they weren't important to you."

She's right. For a moment, Fleance couldn't find words. His face locked down, an automatic response in the face of uncertainty.

Then he realized he didn't need words. He let everything he was feeling flood through the mate bond, and the only thing in the world shining brighter than his emotions were Sheena's eyes.

"What about putting down roots?" he muttered. His voice seemed so inadequate compared to the twin suns of Sheena's gaze.

She tipped her head back and narrowed her eyes mischievously. "What? Right here? With the other trees?" She smiled, wide and lazy and delighted. "I only said I *thought* I'd want to immediately put down roots. I don't. I still want to go and see the world, and have adventures, and see what ridiculous trouble my hellsheep gets me into. I don't just want to go on the trip of a lifetime, I want to have the *life* of a lifetime. With you."

Fleance's hellhound pricked its ears with excitement. Fleance's face hurt, and it took him a moment to realize it was because he was smiling harder than he had in a long time.

"I've still got that plane ticket," Sheena said.

"I can talk to the airline about bringing my return flight forward."

"You can introduce me to your family. I want to meet them. And then…"

"Parker hurt a lot of people in a lot of places," Fleance said gruffly.

"Then we'll go to all those places." Sheena pinched his chin and drew his face down to hers. "And we'll make things right. For them, and for your hellhound."

Fleance carried Sheena's pack back to the house and waited while she rummaged through it for clothes that actually fit her. Sunset hit like a comet, roaring red and gold across the sky and falling into darkness and a bone-deep chill that had everyone except those with something to prove, or a house full of relatives to escape, huddling inside Fiona and Rena's villa.

Outside, Sheena stretched her hands over the hot coals in the abandoned grill, soaking up the last of their warmth. Fleance wrapped his arms around her and frowned at the glowing coals. They pulsed, and new flames flickered up from them.

Sheena sighed contentedly. The sound went straight to Fleance's heart and stuck there, like a dart made of pure light. "Ooh, that's nice. I'll keep you around."

She relaxed into his arms. For a few minutes, there was nothing but the gentle hiss of the flames and the murmur of conversation from the house behind them.

Was it only a few weeks ago I was so worried about my hellhound's behavior that I was jumping at my own shadow? Fleance tipped his head back and looked at the stars blazing in the night sky. Standing here, with his mate, that afternoon with Caine at the Puppy Express felt like a lifetime ago.

Just like his time with Parker felt a lifetime ago, and his world before that another lifetime again. He'd been pulled in so many different directions, and now, finally, he was anchored. Not putting down roots, but secure and whole with the woman who loved him.

A chill breeze ghosted across his face and he thought...

Sheena moved against him. *What are you thinking about?* she asked.

Honestly? Fleance closed his eyes.

Honestly.

Fleance breathed in slowly.

The air was crisp. It stank like rotten eggs, but it held the brisk chill of ice. There was snow on the distant mountains and Fleance was thousands of miles from the only home he'd only known, but in that moment, everything felt perfect.

He pulled Sheena close and kissed the top of her head, breathing her in. Clover honey and wild grass and open skies. But she was more than that, and the proof was all around him. She was wildness and freedom, solitude and endless adventure—and this core of loyalty and love was embodied by her family who'd come from across the country to check on her. Togetherness. Family.

I'm thinking about Christmas again, he admitted.

Because the whole whānau's here? The family, she translated, and tucked his hands into her jacket pockets. *I suppose it is a bit Christmassy. Especially with the barbecue out.*

It's not too cold? I thought Christmas for you meant summer.

She wrinkled her nose. *Of course it's too cold. So? I'm from the South Island. It's not summer unless it's raining.*

It isn't raining now.

She sighed and stared up at the clear, cloudless sky. *It might later.* She kissed him. *Or it might snow. I know it's the middle of the year, but... Happy Un-Christmas, my love.*

Fleance held his mate close. She didn't just let herself be held; she pressed herself against him, as thoughtlessly hungry for his touch as he was for hers. When he closed his eyes and focused on his pack sense, she was his sun; but here, lost in a kiss that filled his heart with light, they circled each other in perfect harmony. His alpha. His mate. The other part of his soul.

And his own soul, whole at last.

Happy Un-Christmas, he whispered, and his hellhound howled with happiness.

EPILOGUE
SHEENA

"This is *torture*," Sheena groaned, pressing her face against the car window.

"I thought I was the one with an inner dog," Fleance laughed. "You want to roll down the window and stick your head out, be my guest."

"Ugh," Sheena groaned. "That'll just make me feel *more* cooped up."

They'd landed in Los Angeles—could it only have been a few days ago? After the twelve-hour flight from Auckland, Sheena's hellsheep had been crazy with cabin fever. Unfortunately, while hellhounds were masters of staying out of sight, hellsheep were apparently not so keen on the idea. Her inner weirdo absolutely refused to let itself turn invisible, so instead of the leisurely days of trying to spy on celebrities that Sheena had planned, she and Fleance had rented a car and headed for the desert. Plenty of wide open spaces for her hellsheep to hoon around in, and, half a day's drive away, a city that a lifetime of watching American media had promised

Sheena would barely notice the presence of giant, fire-breathing livestock: Las Vegas.

And then Fleance had gotten a phone call from his old pack. Something had happened, and they needed all hands on deck.

There had been no time to hoon around the desert. No charging at exciting foreign rocks or finding out if tumbleweeds actually were like in the movies. No acting the wide-eyed tourist on the Strip.

Part of her was glad that Fleance had answered his old pack's call. She had been deadly serious when she said that the people he'd left in Pine Valley sounded like his family, and packing up at a moment's notice and racing to be with your family in their hour of need was what families did... as so recently illustrated by her own fam. Knowing that Fleance felt the same way made her feel soft and warm inside.

And another part of her could not get over the fact that the outside world was right *there*, right outside the window, all green and summery and probably full of delicious things to smell and nibble on and jump on and set on fire and she was *stuck in the car*.

It was a sheepy part of her. But it was still *her*.

She groaned again and stared up at the mountains that filled the sky ahead of them.

"We're a few hours away from Pine Valley still," Fleance said, peering in the same direction. "There are non-shifters living in town, so we still have to be careful, but you'll be able to stretch your legs farther up in the mountains."

A few hours? "Aaargh," Sheena moaned as the open fields either side of the road made way for dense pine forest and they began to wind their way up into the hills. Her hellsheep flared unhappily inside her. *A FEW HOURS? IT'S ALREADY BEEN SO MANY HOURS!*

Twelve on the flight, overnight on the ground without being able to shift, hours and hours squeezed into the car—Sheena couldn't blame her hellsheep for getting antsy.

EXACTLY! it boomed. *AND IT'S NOT LIKE THERE'S ANYONE HERE TO SEE!*

Which was true—the road was pretty empty, out here in the middle of nowhere...

RIGHT, THEN!

"Wait!" Sheena yelped, but it was too late. Her hellsheep shook itself like a dog and took form in a flurry of sparks. She just had time to hear Fleance swear before she dropped through the floor of the car. *Damn it, hellsheep!*

AHHH! SO MUCH BETTER!

Her hellsheep bounded alongside the car, kicking its heels and trailing smoke.

Fleance's voice brushed against her mind. *Sheena?!*

I'm all right! she reassured him quickly. Her hellsheep baa'd with excitement and headbutted a tree. *Um, for a given value of 'all right'...* she amended, feeling dazed. *My hellsheep couldn't take it anymore. It—ow! Seriously? What did the tree ever do to you?*

HAHA! her hellsheep replied, unapologetic.

I can't sense anyone else around here, she told Fleance as her hellsheep slurped in deep breaths of the fresh, green-scented air. *I just—I need to run! Better I get it all out now than when we meet your lot, right?*

He chuckled. *That depends. How likely is your hellsheep to introduce itself by exploding out in the middle of you shaking hands with my old alpha?*

Oh, one hundred percent likelihood, minimum.

In that case I'd better leave you to it.

Sheena barked out laughter. *Like you could stop me!*

I could have fun trying. The mate bond thrummed with promise... but Sheena's hellsheep was having too much fun already.

Later, she said, and Fleance whispered:

I'll hold you to that.

Oh, really? You could have said 'I'll hold that against you' and then I could say 'You can hold me against one of these'—yeek!

She broke off as her hellsheep landed on a fallen tree that immediately collapsed and sent her sprawling into a burbling creek. *I'm fine!* she called to Fleance. She sploshed upstream, water hissing around her hooves. *Still fine!*

Her hellsheep was in heaven. The forest here was mostly pine trees, but they were different varieties to the *pinus radiata* she was familiar with from home. Some had striking white trunks like silver birch or eucalyptus, and all filled the air with a pungent, invigorating scent that reminded Sheena of long summers back home in central Otago.

Long, hay fevery summers.

Her hellsheep sneezed a burst of flame. *Shit!* Sheena thought, and rushed to stomp out the flames before they could spread. *Cool, yep, just burn down the mountain. Perfect way to introduce myself to Fleance's friends and family. Just perfect...*

You still there, babe?

Sheena focused on her pack sense—Fleance was a ways ahead of her, now. The road followed the curve of the mountain and she bounded up until she could see the hire car through the trees. Her nose was still tickling, and if she sneezed another fireball, she figured it might be useful to have another pair of feet nearby to help stomp it out. Or another four feet. Even better.

Bad news, she said, once she felt through the mate bond that Fleance had spotted her. *My hellsheep gets hay fever same as I do.*

Is that just with hay, or…?

Pines. Grass. Anything that's a plant and having a good time being alive. Her hellsheep shook itself and she sniggered as something clicked in her mind. *Now I know what you meant about your heart saying it was Christmas when your head knew it wasn't. I know it's still half a year away, but…*

She closed her eyes and breathed in. The sun on her back, the ground warm and rich underfoot, the smells and lush greenness of all the growing things around her…

This is SO Christmas.

She sneezed again and swore.

And so's that, damn it!

Fleance laughed. *Christmas in the summer seems so upside-down.*

So amazing, you mean. How can you have Christmas without going swimming at the beach? Eating new potatoes with mint and butter, and fresh-caught fish on the barbecue, and a pavlova with strawberries and kiwifruit…

You mean kiwis?

*I mean kiwiFRUIT! You put a kiwi on a pav, you're going to have the Department of Conservation knocking on your door. And that's without even talking about *the most important Christmas tradition of having too much to eat or drink and finding a nice tree outside to take a nap under. How are you meant to have a post-Christmas-dinner nap under a tree in the middle of winter? You'd freeze!*

There's always the Christmas tree. But I thought you said summer where you come from was cold anyway?

Look, if you can't handle a bit of Christmas sleet on your noggin while you sleep off Christmas dinner, then you clearly haven't been celebrating enough. I don't know what to tell you.

But you just said... Fleance groaned. *You're just going to keep talking me in circles, aren't you?*

Am I? It might have been the hay fever, it might have been the sheer joy of running free through the woods and headbutting trees, but Sheena felt drunk. *Is that the sort of thing you might hold against me?*

You'll have to wait and see.

Aww...

The sun curved down across the sky as they made their way up into the mountains. The light turned golden, as though the whole world was covered in a fine layer of pollen—which from Sheena's perspective, it might as well have been.

It's beautiful up here, she said. *I've always loved mountains.*

Something bright and hopeful flickered down the mate bond. *We haven't talked about... maybe

once we've run out of wanderlust, and things to fix...
Fleance's voice was hesitant.

Sheena leaped onto an outcrop of rock that gave her a view back down the mountain. The landscape was wonderfully crumpled, and all covered in dense forest. She turned to peer further up wherever the road was leading and saw the distant shine of the late-afternoon sun reflecting off what had to be the roofs and windows of Pine Valley-the-town, as opposed   to Pine-Valley-accurate-description-of-every-valley-she'd-run-through-so-far.

She was half a world away from home, and she had no idea what she'd find in the forest as she explored it further, or whether she'd like Fleance's family and they'd like her, and she had a *lot* of wanderlust left, but...

Maybe, she agreed, and darted back to the road in time to see the worry on Fleance's face melt into delight.

A few minutes later, her nose wasn't the only thing that was tickling.

The wool on the back of her neck was prickling, as though someone was looking at her. Her hellsheep spun around several times, yelling *HAH!*, but there was no one there.

Do you sense anyone around? she asked Fleance, who was a hundred meters or so back down the road.

He paused before answering, and she could feel the care he put into checking their surroundings. *...Nothing close,* he said at last.

Further up the mountain? Or behind us? But that didn't make sense. If she could feel someone watching her, they must be *close*, not so far up or down the mountain that Fleance couldn't clearly sense them. Unless...

She looked up. Something flickered in the sky far above the treetops.

Is that a bird?

Fleance pulled over and craned his neck out the car window. "That's not a bird," he called over to her, just as the creature's wings flared out and caught the late-afternoon sun.

FLEANCE

Fleance swore as he saw the flying creature's wings glitter like black diamonds. "What the hell is he doing flying so far down the mountain?" he muttered to himself and reached out telepathically. Hopefully the kid wasn't too far away...

Cole, he began warningly, just as Sheena's voice exploded in his head.

It's a DRAGON! she yelled. *I can't believe it! A real dragon!*

"A real dumbass kid of a dragon," Fleance grumbled. "Where are his parents? What are Hank and Opal thinking, letting him—"

He cut himself off, fully aware that it likely wasn't a case of the Heartwells 'letting' their son fly out of the safe zone so much as a case of them turning their backs for the split second necessary for Cole to decide to stretch his wings.

Cole swooped closer, then canted his wings so he was hovering above the treetops. *Oh, darn, you spotted me!* he cried.

A blind mole could spot you flying out in the open like that, Fleance told him, and then realized Cole wasn't angling his descent towards him. He was heading for the bursts of movement and shimmery flames where Sheena's hellsheep was doing as poor a job of staying hidden as the dragonling was.

Hey, Cole… Fleance began. The last thing he wanted was the kid freaking out when he realized he was about to land in front of a stranger.

WHEEE!

Another voice chimed like a bell in his head, and Fleance's chest seized up. Oh, God. Cole wasn't the only rogue dragonling flying down the mountain: his little cousin, Ruby, was here as well, her brilliant red wings shining like her namesake as she did loops in the air.

Oh, God, Fleance thought. His hellhound was paralyzed inside him. *Both of them?*

He couldn't fight the feeling that everything was about to go terribly wrong. Sheena was a stranger, of a shifter type no one in Pine Valley had ever seen before. Anyone who saw her wouldn't see the sweet, infuriating woman he'd fallen for so suddenly and completely—they'd see a giant sheep with smoke pouring from her woolen coat, who was literally sneezing fire.

And the other thing they would see was him.

Not Fleance, who'd run into a burning building to save a woman he'd just met. Not the Fleance who'd stayed by that woman's side as she defeated the most evil man he'd ever known, and who had finally found a pack and a place for himself that felt right.

They would see Flea. Hopeless Flea. Dangerous Flea. Flea who set fires, and hurt people, not saved them. Flea who couldn't control his hellhound when faced with people who were breaking the rules...

...and two dragonlings taking a joyride down the mountain definitely counted as breaking the rules.

He could see it all unrolling, scene by scene. Cole and Ruby startled by Sheena. Him trying to reassure them, and it only getting worse, because of course the Heartwells would have warned their children away from him. And if any of the adults turned up…

His mouth went dry as his psychic senses pricked, alerting him to several shifter presences right at the edge of his awareness.

Sheena, he began, his voice halting, *it might be best to shift back for this.*

Oh, no, really? I'm not sure my hellsheep bothered to bring my clothes with me this shift, and I don't want to introduce myself to your friends in my birthday suit…

He tried to keep his feelings under control, but a tendril slithered out along the mate bond.

Sheena paused. *Wait, you're seriously worried about this, aren't you? What's wrong?* She yanked on the mate bond, and Fleance had a sudden vision of her pulling it up to her eyes and inspecting it. *Tell me what's the matter, and I'll—*

A booming echo replaced her voice in his mind, all he could hear of what was her hellsheep no doubt making terrible threats. The opposite of what he needed. He hurried out of the car.

Cole, Ruby, he called warningly. *I'm over here!*

It's cool, I see you! Cole yelled back, flying in the wrong direction. *In the woods!*

No, I'm back here, on the— On the road. His brain seized. Was he really about to ask two shifted dragonlings to meet him on the main road into

town? What if one of Pine Valley's human residents
drove past?

Before he could unfreeze, Ruby barreled into Cole
in midair and they both dropped down through the
canopy. A shriek cut through the air. Fleance broke
through his fears and ran.

His hellhound bristled beneath his skin, half
desperate to break out and run faster towards Sheena
and the dragonlings, half cringing with guilt and
misery with the knowledge that that would make
him seem like more of a threat.

Ahead of him, branches cracked. Smoke billowed.
Shrill dragonling voices shrieked and roared. He
burst through into the clearing that his pack sense
told him was where Sheena was, expecting the
worst, and found—

Sheena laughing in delight. Smoke puffed out of
her mouth. *You're a lot smaller than I thought dragons
would be,* she said to Cole, who was standing in
front of her, jaw hanging open. *And YOU'RE even
smaller!* she added, craning her neck to look at the
tiny bright-red dragon clinging to her back.

You're not Flea, Cole said, shrinking down.

Sheena laughed. *No, I'm Sheena! I'm a hellsheep
shifter! What's your name?*

Umm... Cole murmured, but Ruby jumped up,
wings spread wide and tail whipping back and
forth. Fleance's chest relaxed. Sure, Cole had gone

suddenly shy, but he wasn't freaking out. Maybe this wasn't going to be a disaster after all.

CAN BREAV FIRE! Ruby crowed, and demonstrated.

Or maybe it still was, he thought, as a nearby bush caught fire.

WOW! WHAT A POWERFUL DRAGON! Sheena boomed. *Er, I mean, oh dear! That's very cool but very unsafe, too! Fleance!*

Fleance ran over as she tried to stomp out the fire.

Flea! Cole piped up happily. *I thought I saw you but it was this lady instead!*

"What are you two doing this far down the mountain?" Fleance asked, half-distracted as he helped Sheena stamp on the flames.

Um... Cole said again, twiddling his foreclaws innocently.

Oh, sh—sheesh. Fleance, this isn't working! Sheena's voice was tight. *Look!*

She stomped on a burning branch—and it caught fire more.

It's my hellsheep! Sheena all but wailed. *It thinks this is FUN!*

BIG FIRE! Ruby chirped, and belched out another fireball from her seat on Sheena's back. Sheena spun round and made the fire bigger as she tried to squash it.

Oh, come ON, hellsheep! she yelled.

A shadow passed over the clearing and the hairs on the back of Fleance's neck stood on end.

Some help here, Fleance! Sheena called out, half-laughing. He barely heard her. *Oh, sh—*

Oh no, Fleance's hellhound muttered. Fleance was already tense; now he felt like his bones were about to crack under the strain. *What?*

They're here…

More dragons! Sheena squeaked. *More… bigger dragons! Oh, God, Fleance, I hope no one but you heard that.*

The whole Heartwell clan was there. Cole's parents: Opal, with her shining iridescent scales, and Hank, who was classic dragon green. Jasper Heartwell, Opal's brother and Ruby's father, had scales the same multitude of colors as his gemstone namesake, shimmering oranges and reds and browns. The three dragons folded their wings and landed, twining their long, sinuous bodies between the trees without disturbing a single branch.

Hey, kiddos, Jasper said, and Ruby trilled with excitement. She leaped off Sheena's back and flapped towards her dad, who caught her in one clawed hand. *Having fun, firecracker? Who are your new friends?*

Movement at the corner of Fleance's eye made him twitch around. He put a warning hand on Sheena's hellsheep's shoulder.

Shadows were pouring through the trees. They resolved into three hellhounds. Rhys was wiry and thin, Manu pure tank, and Caine was all alpha, twice the size of the others. Fleance's pack—except not anymore. He had been so distracted by the dragons he hadn't even sensed their approach.

Hello again, Flea. Caine sounded—not unkind, or wary, but exhausted. If he'd been in human form Fleance could imagine him rubbing his forehead. *You got my message? I wasn't expecting you back so soon.*

There was a tinge of guilt in his voice, and before Fleance could decode it, Caine stepped between him and Cole.

"We were already in the country," Fleance said, trying to sound confident. It came out as half a growl.

The edges of his mind buzzed: a hurried psychic conversation was going on, without his involvement.

He didn't need to hear what they were saying to know what they were talking about. It was obvious the moment the other shifters' stances turned from casual-bordering-on-wary to defensive.

Huh? Sheena murmured.

Flea—it's fine. The dragonlings were just playing. They're not endangering themselves or anyone else.

Caine's voice was pure alpha. Controlled, with the burn of a warning beneath each word.

Other voices filled his mind, jagged-edged. Voices not meant for him, but the shifters who were speaking were too panicked to keep their telepathy private.

Remember what happened at the Puppy Express—

He chased that fraternity group all the way to Sweetheart Lake before you caught up with him—

Kids! Get behind me, now!

All the blood drained from Fleance's body. The Heartwells, his old pack—they weren't happy to see him. They were afraid.

Cole stared at his parents, confused, and looked back at Fleance uncertainly. Fire flickered behind him.

Setting forest fires in the middle of summer. Talk about breaking all the rules meant to protect people and the land they lived on.

Everything he knew they thought about him pounded against his mind. *Dangerous—untrustworthy—weak—*

The mate bond strained like a kite string in a storm, and Sheena pulled it taut.

Fleance—what? No. You're none of those things. You know that. I know that. She leaned into his touch and shifted. *And if anyone here thinks otherwise...*

In human form again, she looked slightly singed around the edges, with one shoe and the hem of her shirt missing, but she didn't pay any attention to how much of her clothes she'd been able to shift back with.

He met her eyes. She wasn't afraid, or panicking, or horrified. Her excitement at meeting dragons and his old pack, and embarrassment at all the fires, and concern for him, all poured through the mate bond—and met his rising terror halfway there.

Her eyebrows snapped down and Fleance's breath cracked as she trampled his terror beneath a flood of love. *Don't be afraid*, the light connecting his heart to hers seemed to say; *there's nothing to be afraid of here. Not with your mate beside you.*

Fleance's hellhound raised its head. He straightened his shoulders. The fire all around them crackled against his senses and suddenly, his power twisted inside him, fueled by Sheena's faith in him.

He lifted one hand and closed his fist. The fire died.

Now that's new. The largest hellhound shimmered and transformed into Caine, who walked forwards, hands in pockets. His eyes searched Fleance's and he frowned. "So your hellhound—wait. I don't understand. Why can't I sense you in the pack anymore?"

Fleance was surprised at how easily a smile came to his face. Then again, with Sheena's love like the sun in his chest, maybe he shouldn't have been. He put one arm around her and pulled her close.

"I'm afraid that's my fault," Sheena said, with more than a trace of smugness in her voice. She put a possessive hand over his on her waist.

Caine looked at them both, and the exhausted wariness on his face relaxed into a smile. "I'm glad to hear it. Caine Guinness." He extended one hand and Sheena took it.

"I'm—" she began, and Ruby let out a shriek of excitement.

FIRE SHEEP! she screamed, and even the full-grown dragons winced at the force of her psychic voice. Then she leaped out of Jasper's claws. *COME BACK! BREAV MORE FIRE!*

Firecracker, no! Jasper yelled, and she shrieked unhappily and belched fire into his face. Jasper swore, and then made a strangled oh-God-I-swore-in-front-of-my-toddler noise. *Firecracker, spitting fire at people isn't very nice…*

Behind him, Opal rolled her pearlescent eyes. *Maybe if you gave her a different nickname…*

Fleance clenched one fist. The fire went out. "It's fine, it's not a—"

NOOO! MY FIIIIIRES! NOT FAIIIIR! Ruby howled, and threw herself onto the ground. Which she immediately set on fire.

Why are you complaining? Cole piped up. He flicked his tail at Fleance. *He can make the fire stop, right? So there's nothing to worry about!* He punctuated this speech by sending a rope of flame shooting towards a tree Ruby was heading towards. She shrieked and aimed her next fireball at his head. He ducked, and another tree caught fire.

Fleance stepped up before anyone else could move, and extinguished the fires.

"OK, kids, I get you're having fun and all, but—"

WANNA HAVE ADVENTURE! WANNA FIRE!

"You can't just—"

Giggles filled his mind. Sheena was doubled over with strangled laughter. She bit her lip as their eyes met. *At least I'm not the one setting everything on fire?* she said, and covered her face as she gave in to laughter. "Oh, God, Fleance, it looks like we came back at just the right moment after all."

"It… does," Caine said slowly. He looked Fleance up and down. Fleance shot him a distracted smile and snuffed another fire. For a power he'd only learned how to use a minute ago, he was sure getting a lot of practice.

Cole whined something about it not being *fair* that he had to share his adventure with his cousin, which turned out to be a feint to distract his parents as Ruby tried to make her escape. Jasper hauled off after her in human form, his dragon form too big to follow her between the trees. Rhys yelped a warning as another fire kindled beneath Hank's tail.

And in the middle of it all, Caine laughed.

Fleance clenched his fist again, snuffing another patch of fire, and stared at him in amazement.

"I was worried, but... You sorted out your problem, then?" Caine asked, wiping his eyes.

Fleance looked around. Rule-breaking and havoc abounded, and his hellhound wasn't rearing to lay down the law—it was ready to jump in and cause some havoc of its own.

And there was Sheena. Still laughing. As though she sensed him watching her—and of course she did—she lifted one hand and pointed behind him. He sensed fire brewing in a dragonling's nostrils without having to look and extinguished Ruby's fireball with a smirk.

Not a smirk like Parker would make when he looked out over the results of his latest con job, or the paralyzed, rigid expression Fleance and his packmates would find plastered to their faces as they tried not to let their true feelings show. A full-hearted, absolutely smug and glorious smirk at the knowledge that it would never again be just him against the world and all of the dangers in it. It would be him, and Sheena, together, and whatever dangers they faced, they outmatched them by far.

"Yes, I sorted it out. And then some," he told Caine.

When the forest was once again fire-free, Fleance and Sheena piled back into the car and drove the rest of the way up the mountain. The dragons peeled off into the clouds before they reached town, leaving Sheena, Fleance and the other hellhounds on the road to the Guinnesses' property.

The Guinnesses lived in a stone and wood house surrounded by forest. Fleance had first seen it in the winter, when he, Rhys and Manu had slunk up to Caine and Meaghan's doorstep to beg a place in their pack. Then, it had looked like something out of a fairy tale, glowing warm and bright amid the snow-covered pines and dark, icy night.

Now, mid-summer, it was as though that magic had seeped out to color the house's surroundings. Pale new growth tipped the branches of the trees, and small flowers clustered around the house's foundations and patchworked the yard.

But none of that was what made Fleance's stomach flip as he got out of the car. He looked across at Sheena as she stepped out onto the drive, and she raised her eyebrows. Did she feel it, too?

He and Sheena weren't the only new thing in town. No wonder Caine's message had been so tense.

Caine was already there, sitting on his haunches in front of the house. When Fleance and Sheena got out of the car, he shifted back to human form, and cleared his throat.

"You must be wondering why I didn't come after you to help sort out Parker," Caine said.

Fleance hadn't. He'd thought it was up to him, alone, but somehow, standing here in front of his old alpha's house with his new pack bond bright inside him and the echo of the Guinnesses' pack bond running over everything he could see was giving him a new perspective. He could see at last how much this place had felt like home, even when he didn't trust himself, or believe he deserved a home.

Sheena slipped her hand into his and squeezed it.

"Is it all right that I'm here?" she asked Caine. "I mean—I can feel this is the heart of your pack. Somehow. Is there a ceremony, or…?"

Caine looked flummoxed. "God knows. But you're welcome here, of course you are. Both of you. Pack or not, Fleance, you're one of us, and your mate is, too."

"You need to get started writing that manual," Fleance joked.

"That sounds like a task I could hand off to you, now," he replied, grimacing.

Sheena asked what they were talking about, and when Fleance explained, snorted. "*I'll* write the manual, and then you'll both be sorry."

"Please. Both of you come in, and—" Caine took a deep breath and gestured helplessly. "I don't want you to think I abandoned you. Meaghan was onto me to go after you as soon as Rhys and Manu let slip where you'd gone. She was right. Or maybe she was just sick of me trailing after her like an anxious puppy. But things happened—early, not too early, but sudden. Opal came at once, of course, and she'd helped Abigail when Ruby was born, so she knew what she was doing, but it was still…"

Sheena gave Fleance a worried look. He had a strong suspicion he looked petrified, himself. Then Meaghan, Caine's mate, called from inside the house:

"For God's sake, Caine! Stop terrifying them and bring them inside!"

It was the most terrifying moment of my life, Caine muttered to Fleance as he opened the front door for them.

Meaghan was in the living room, ensconced in a throw rug with the sun streaming in and turning her dark curls into a halo around her head.

She smiled as Fleance and Sheena came in. "He fainted," was the first thing she said, and Caine groaned out loud. "Not that I'm meant to tell you that. Protecting his alpha dignity, et cetera."

"You were just glad I got myself out of the way," Caine accused her, ducking to kiss her on the forehead.

"The floor isn't 'out of the way'!" she grumbled. It sounded like a well-worn conversation. Fleance barely heard it.

He was speechless. If he needed any more proof that Caine trusted him, this was it. Tucked up in Meaghan's lap were two tiny babies, their scrunched-up faces and fluffy tufts of hair enough to break any shifter's heart.

"Meet Lola and Hamish," Meaghan said, as Caine slipped onto the sofa beside her and took one of the twins. "The newest members of our pack—but... not your pack, anymore?" She stared hard at Fleance, as though she was trying to look inside him, then blinked and rubbed her forehead. "It might just be the sleep deprivation talking, but..."

Fleance was speechless again. Meaghan was human; so far as he'd been aware, she'd never been able to sense the pack bonds before. But Abigail Heartwell was human, too, and she'd said that after she had Ruby, she had been able to connect to her daughter psychically. Maybe the same was true with hellhound mothers, with added pack sense?

Caine picked up her hand from her forehead and kissed it. "You're right," she told her. "He's broken the pack bond somehow."

"By forming another." Fleance was surprised. His voice didn't come out choked, or surly. It was warm and heady with pride. "Sheena, this is Meaghan, Caine's mate. Meaghan—Sheena Mackay. My mate, and the reason Parker isn't going to be a danger to your family or anyone else, ever again."

Meaghan's eyes lit up. "So, you're your own alpha now?"

"Well…" He exchanged a look with Sheena. "That depends. What day is it?"

"Meet-your-family day," she murmured. "Which means you're in charge."

She narrowed her eyes at him, and power tugged deliciously under his skin as they each tested one another's authority. Sheena pushed up onto her tiptoes and nipped him on the chin. "And no take-backs," she warned him.

Not until tonight, he replied, and she blushed bright red.

"Lunch!" Meaghan announced, and there was a flurry of activity from the direction of the kitchen. Fleance cast out his senses and found Rhys and Manu. Meaghan grinned. "If I don't give them anything to do, they default to standing around staring at me and the babies like they're terrified we're going to shatter into a million pieces."

"Or call up absent members of the pack to join the vigil," Caine said, suitably abashed. He nodded at Fleance. "If my message sounded a bit panicked…"

"It's because he is panicking. Constantly." Meaghan sighed dramatically, then met Fleance's eyes. "You said Parker isn't a danger anymore?"

Fleance quickly explained, with Sheena backing him up, that Parker had lost his alpha powers and wouldn't be able to hurt anyone else. That he would never set foot in Pine Valley again.

"Good." Meaghan closed her eyes briefly. "That was the one thing that was panicking *me*. If he's dealt with…" Her gaze softened as she looked down at her babies, then at Caine. "This feels a lot like happy ever after," she said quietly.

Power tugged beneath Fleance's skin again, and he looked down at Sheena. Without speaking, they moved to the edge of the room, letting the hellhound alpha and his mate have their private moment.

And giving them the space to have one for themselves. Sheena blushed, and tipped her head back. *Seeing them like this… I don't know,* she whispered, shaking her head.

Makes you want to be in charge again?

She slipped her arms around his waist. *Makes me want to have as much to protect as they do.*

Excitement leaped in Fleance's heart and her eyebrows drew together, mock-severe.

After traveling the world. And showing you what a real New Zealand Christmas is like. And kicking Parker's arse some more. And—we can't do it all at once, can we?

Can't we?

As he kissed her, Fleance thought for the first time in his life that maybe, just maybe, he could have everything his heart desired.

MORE PARANORMAL ROMANCE BY ZOE CHANT

A Mate for Christmas

A Mate for the Christmas Dragon
Christmas Hellhound
Christmas Pegasus
The Hellhound's UnChristmas Miracle
Christmas Griffin

A Gift for the Christmas Dragon (novella)

Shifter Suspense

Claimed by the Panther
Saved by the Billionaire Lion Shifter
Stealing the Snow Leopard's Heart
Craving the Kraken
Falling for the Shadow Dragon
Seducing the Soul-Eater

Hideaway Cove

The Griffin's Mate
The Sea Wolf's Mate
The Lightning Dragon's Mate
The Duskfire Dragon's Mate
The Kelpie's Mate

Standalone books not in series

Her Purr-fect Christmas Mate
Trusting the Tiger
Bear With Me

MONSTER ROMANCE BY MARIE CARDNO

The Monster Girlfriend series